To God be the [...]
Jessie Gussman I Cor 10:31

D1536269

Heartland Gold

A Heartland Cowboy Christmas

Jessie Gussman

Published by Jessie Gussman, 2021.

This is a work of fiction. Similarities to real people, places, or events are entirely coincidental.

HEARTLAND GOLD

First edition. October 15, 2021.

Copyright © 2021 Jessie Gussman.

Written by Jessie Gussman.

Cover art by Julia Gussman
Editing by Heather Hayden[1]
Narration by Jay Dyess[2]
Proofreading by Tandy O from Eagle Eye Proofreading

~~~

Click HERE[3] if you'd like to subscribe to my newsletter and find out why people say "Jessie's is the only newsletter I open and read."

~~~

1.   https://hhaydeneditor.com/
2.   https://www.facebook.com/SayWithJay
3. https://BookHip.com/FASFD

Chapter 1

Keene Emerson turned off his pickup and pushed the door open against the gusting Iowa wind.

The trailer park on the outskirts of Prairie Rose was barren and brown this time of year, just a few weeks before Christmas.

A few Christmas decorations were scattered through the area, but in order to stay where they had been placed, they had to be anchored quite firmly.

Most of them hadn't been.

He slammed his door closed and stared for just a second at the trailer in front of him.

It might have been light blue at one point, but it was now a faded gray. The steps leaned awkwardly, and the small platform at the top of them didn't seem to be attached to the trailer.

A swift swirl of apprehension surprised him, and he tightened his abdominal muscles instinctively, getting rid of it.

He hadn't talked to Shelby Yingling much since they'd graduated from high school. She'd been a nice girl, smart, but the opposite of everything he was.

He wouldn't have guessed that she would have ended up like this, though.

A single mom with three small children living with her mother in a trailer park, and from what he'd heard from the folks at church, working two jobs to try to make ends meet.

He strode up the rickety steps, hoping the small, wobbly platform held his weight, and knocked firmly on the door.

The church had donated lumber and material to add a room onto the back of her trailer. Since her husband had taken off two years ago, her mother had come to live with them, and according to the ladies at church, Shelby had been sleeping on the couch all that time, giving her mother her bedroom.

Another gust of wind rustled the brown leaves of corn left in the field adjacent to the trailer park.

Keene couldn't hear whether there were footsteps in the trailer or not, so he knocked again.

There was no car parked next to the trailer, but even if Shelby were working, her mother should be home. At least the ladies at the church seemed to think someone would be home since this was the time they'd told him to come out with the lumber and also with the Christmas packages that had been donated for the children.

He had lived in Iowa his entire life, so the cold, biting wind was not a shock even as it seeped through his jacket and curled around his neck.

After the heat of the summer, the chill of winter always took a little bit of getting used to.

If he was going to put this addition on, he'd be working in the cold wind, so he willed his body to hurry up and get acclimated.

Raising his hand to knock for the third time, not wanting to take the load of lumber that was on the trailer hooked to the back of his pickup home to his farm, he said a quick prayer that someone was home as his hand came down to rap on the door.

Before it hit the cheap material, the door pulled open, and a woman who looked like she'd just gotten out of bed, stood in front of him.

Her hair was wild and in complete disarray around her face. One side of her cheek was red and creased like she'd been sleeping on it and it had wrinkled up under her head.

She wore what looked like long underwear, and her feet were bare.

"Do you need something?" the woman said, her eyes blinking like she still hadn't quite woken up and was trying to figure out what in the world someone was doing standing at her front door.

"I'm Keene Emerson," Keene said, hesitating for just a moment before holding out his hand. It seemed like a formal gesture, considering the lady's attire, but it made the fact that he didn't seem to be wanted a little less relevant. For some reason. "I'm here from the church. They had talked to you about the addition that they are going to put on your house?"

The woman looked at his hand, her eyes widening just a touch, before she seemed to pull herself up. Her hand came up, warm and rougher than he would have guessed, slipping into his.

"I'm Shelby Yingling. Used to be Shelby Henniger. I knew you from high school."

He nodded. He figured that's who she was; although, sometimes it was dangerous to make assumptions, and he hadn't wanted to do that.

"I'm sorry. I forgot all about the room the church said they'd be donating. That was this summer when someone had approached me about it. Are you here to see where it's going to go?" she asked as though she hadn't heard or processed his earlier statements.

Her brows were drawn over her eyes, and he opened his mouth to answer her, but his own gaze kind of got caught on those eyes.

Blue, a sweet, light blue. Like the sky in September. A sky with no clouds, no haze, just a brilliant, true blue. Somehow, they were penetrating.

He gave his head a mental shake and pulled his hand away from hers. Her hand had almost as many calluses as his, and it was disconcerting, especially coupled with her eyes.

He almost laughed out loud at himself. Her eyes were disconcerting. Whether or not he was touching her hand.

"I'm sorry. I wasn't in charge of calling you, I was just in charge of bringing it. So, no, I'm not here to talk about it, necessarily. I'm here to deliver the materials that have been purchased." He paused. "But I'm probably the one who's going to be building it, so if you have time and want to, we can certainly talk about what you'd like done. Although, I'm not starting today." He added that last bit just so she wouldn't be confused.

Dorothy, one of the older ladies at church, had wrangled his assent to take her granddaughter out this evening.

Keene hadn't been too interested, but Dorothy had been insistent. Keene hadn't wanted to say a firm no because he'd known Dorothy all his life and she was a sweet, kind lady, whom he respected. Even though he highly doubted he was going to hit it off with Lacey, who was from Linglestown, a larger town to the south, and daughter of the mayor there. From what he understood, she was used to the finer things in life.

He loved finer things, but that wasn't his life.

Still, a commitment was a commitment, and he wasn't going to be starting any additions today.

Shelby looked around, squeezing her eyes closed, almost as though they were sore, and then shaking her head, she turned back to him. "I'm sorry. I'm not sure what time it is."

Keene pulled his phone out of his pocket. "It's almost three o'clock."

He had probably an hour he could spend here before he had to go home and get the barn work done so he'd be cleaned up in time to pick up Lacey at seven.

He'd suggested going out much earlier, but apparently that's not the way it was done. At least in Lacey's mind, because the five o'clock he'd suggested had made her gasp.

"Okay." Shelby nodded, like she'd come to a decision. "If we can be quiet, because Perry is still sleeping."

"That must be one of your children?"

"Yeah." Her brows came down again, and she shook her head a little, confused. "It's weird that you know so much about me and I don't know anything about you."

"All I know is that you must have kids, because I have some gifts in the back of my truck that the church has donated for Christmas. I was supposed to deliver those as well. And I only know about the addition because I was commissioned to bring the materials out, and I've also volunteered to build it. As far as I know, I'm the only volunteer."

He had known her name and was pretty sure they'd gone to school together, but that was about the extent of his knowledge. Other than her husband had left her.

"I'm sorry. I worked last night and didn't get off until dinnertime today. I'm going back in this evening, and I was trying to catch a little bit of sleep." She gave a humorless laugh. "I'm sure you've noticed I'm a little groggy."

"It's totally understandable. Especially if you worked last night."

Those eyes looked up at him, and he almost lost his train of thought, but he grabbed it and continued on. "During harvest season, I've worked twenty-four-hour days and spent more than one long night in the combine. It really messes with your internal clock."

She nodded, her face holding the look of someone who was relieved that the person she was talking to seemed to understand her.

The wind gusted again, and she crossed her arms over her chest. "You can come on in, although, please be quiet, and if you don't mind waiting for a minute while I throw some clothes on, I can show you what they were thinking with the addition."

"If you tell me where to put the gifts, I'll unload the pickup while you're getting dressed." He hesitated just a moment before saying "getting dressed." He supposed, technically, she was standing in front of him in her underwear. Even if it was long underwear.

It was a little disconcerting.

"Gifts? That's right. I guess you did say gifts. Wow. I wasn't expecting..."

Keene shifted uncomfortably, the platform under his feet wobbling worryingly, as her eyes seemed to fill with tears.

He hadn't been around too many people who cried, other than the occasional upset child; in fact, he wasn't sure he'd ever been around an adult who cried.

His hands started to sweat. And he hoped her tears wouldn't spill. He wouldn't know what to do.

Was it rude to stand and watch someone while they cried?

But he didn't really know her well enough to even pat her back, let alone try to hug her.

Thankfully, she lifted her chin and said, "We can put them in my mother's bedroom. As long as we're quiet. Do you want me to help you carry them in?"

"No. I can do it, just tell me where to go with them and... Is it okay if I walk in with my boots on?"

He'd been to a couple of people's houses who were kinda fussy about it, but he was wearing his work boots, which had to be untied before he could take them off, and it was a little more involved than if he just had sneakers or cowboy boots on. But he didn't want to disrespect her house.

"That's fine," she said, shaking her head and waving her hand a little as though it was the least of her worries.

He almost smiled. Someone who had worked all night and through dinnertime and was going back in to work tonight certainly must have more important things to worry about than whether or not someone took their shoes off before they went in their house.

"Her room is down that hall right there. There'll be a bathroom on the left, but just keep going. Ignore the bucket of water in the hall from the leaking roof. I haven't had a chance to empty it. And you don't need to knock on the door although it's probably closed."

"Do I need to hide them?" he asked, not wanting to spoil any surprises. Also taking note of the leaking roof. He should fix that while he was putting the addition on. "How long has the roof been leaking?" The words were out before he could stop them.

Her head jerked toward him at his last question, but it was too late to take it back.

"A while. I know I need to get it fixed." She didn't elaborate, but if she was working as much as she seemed to be, she probably didn't have the time or the money. "As for the gifts. No. I'll take care of them. Probably tomorrow I'll take them out to the shed, but I need to make room for them first. Mom is shopping with Grace and Haley, and they'll be back, but I'll text her and let her know not to go in her room just in case she gets back before I'm done showing you around."

"Sounds good." He turned to go back out, walking carefully down the steps and making a mental note to himself that maybe he should get a few lengths of treated lumber and strengthen the steps so they didn't wobble every time someone shifted on them. A couple of brackets might be helpful to attach them to the trailer as well.

Taking a look at her roof would probably be too nosy today, but when he was putting the addition on, he'd need to do some roofing anyway, so he could check it out then.

He pulled his phone back out of his pocket and pulled up the notes section, jotting a few words down and leaving it up just in case he needed to take notes when she showed him how to lay out the addition.

He hadn't done construction for a living, but over the winter most years, he'd worked for his cousin's crew when things got slow around the farm. Their laying houses was year-round work, but they obviously didn't have crops to take care of in the winter. And his brother Elias typically did the maintenance on the farm machinery during that downtime.

It took three trips to carry all the gifts in, and he tried to be careful not to drag any dirt in with them each time. Shelby looked like she was up to her earlobes in work, and he didn't want to add to her load.

There was something about her that just tugged at his heartstrings. Maybe it was the fact that she was working so much, or maybe it was those eyes, but he could hardly look at her and not want to help her as much as he possibly could.

Of course, that was partly his nature, which was why he was here volunteering to put an addition on a stranger's home, or, if not exactly a stranger, someone he'd not talked to more than a couple times in the last decade.

By the time he was done carrying the gifts in, she had reappeared from the other end of the trailer, dressed in jeans and a sweatshirt and carrying boots, which she stuck on before motioning him to follow her back out the door.

The platform at the top of the steps was even more tiny and wobbly with two people on it, and he was more than a little concerned that both of them were going to end up in a heaping pile of rubble on the ground.

But they managed to make it down without it collapsing, and with a glance over her shoulder to make sure he was coming, she walked around the other end of the trailer.

Chapter 2

Shelby led the way around her single-wide trailer, and she felt like she was finally waking up.

She still couldn't quite believe it. One of the Emerson brothers, Keene, the one who had been her age in school, was at her house and wanting to build an addition.

He'd brought gifts for the children.

He was just an ambassador for the church. And she was most definitely indebted to the church. She didn't even go. She worked on Sunday mornings and hadn't been to church in years.

The kindness of the Prairie Rose community had shaken her. Shocked her. And humbled her even though she'd grown up here.

She'd never thought she'd be the kind of person who would need help like this.

But despite—or because of—her degree in art history, she hadn't been able to find a good-paying job, and through bad luck and bad decisions, she'd ended up where she was. Not where she planned to be.

Now, she was just trying to hold everything together. Which was harder than it sounded.

"When the pastor was out, and he'd mentioned it, we talked about having the room come off of this back door." She pointed to the back door, supposing they could have walked out of it, but the trailer had felt claustrophobic with Keene in it, and she'd not wanted him to walk across her living room. "I think he'd said it would be eight by twelve. Which will fit on our lot."

She stopped and gestured from the door to the approximate area where they had measured out and decided the room would fit. Now, she turned to Keene. "There can't be any kind of foundation. We can put a hole in the trailer if we want to, since I own it. But the lot is rented, and I can't put a permanent structure on it."

"I see." He didn't say anything else, and she wasn't sure whether he had been planning on putting in a foundation or not. Probably not, but she had wanted to be clear.

"I'm not sure what materials you have or what details you talked about, but there wasn't going to be a door to the outside although there was going to be a window in each wall."

"That's what I'd heard. I actually don't have the windows, but I have all the lumber to frame everything out. I'll need to get the roofing and the siding and the windows once we have the frame up. It won't take long."

"Really?" In her mind, she'd been thinking it would be done next summer sometime. If then.

"Sure. It should be finished before Christmas. Although, I've been hearing rumors of a big storm coming. I can work inside during that but probably won't be framing anything or putting roofing or siding on. So if I don't have the outside done, I won't be able to work."

"I heard the same rumors last night at work." Working at the convenience store, she saw a lot of different people, and since she was the manager of the night shift, her pay was a little more than average.

Unfortunately, her other job was minimum-wage menial labor, but she had bills to pay, and she'd take whatever job she could get.

Someday... Someday maybe she'd actually get a degree that would enable her to get a good job. Art history had been a terrible choice. It wasn't good for too many things, especially not in the middle of Iowa.

"I can't start tonight," Keene said.

"I understand. You have farm work to do, of course. I appreciate you even taking the time to do this."

"Yeah," he said a little uncertainly, like maybe it wasn't farm work that was keeping him from coming, but he didn't say anything more.

"Are there other people who are going to help you?"

"I'll probably rope my brothers into some of it—although Preston's going to be staying with Gram who is having an operation. Nothing serious," he said quickly. He must have seen her mouth open and the concern on her face. Everyone knew Miss Matilda and loved her. "Just any operation at her age has risks, and Preston's going to be staying with her, taking care of her. Braxton and his wife have a new baby, plus they just moved into their new home. And that leaves Elias, who just got married."

"I'd heard that. I was happy for them. I knew Catherine in school although she was a little older than I was, and she was always so nice."

"Yeah. She's like one of the family to us, and I know they're going to be happy together."

"I wasn't really thinking of your brothers when I asked, though. The church is donating, and I thought maybe some men from there might be helping. It just seems like it shouldn't be all Emerson responsibility." She knew it was a pride thing, but she hated being beholden to anyone, and this seemed like a lot for any one man or even family to do.

"Maybe a few people will pitch in. But being that it's around the holidays, everyone seems to be pretty busy."

"I didn't mean to sound ungrateful or like people should be helping. It's so generous of the church to donate this and so very generous of you to donate your time." She didn't want to explain about the pride thing. It was silly of her to even think that way. She tried to infuse some excitement into her voice. "This is so exciting, and I can't believe that it's actually going to be done before Christmas. Maybe." She added that last since he had just said he was hoping but wasn't sure, and she didn't want him to feel pressure to be finished.

"I'll do my best. I'm sure that you all are cramped in there. Three kids, right?" His question was a little hesitant as though he didn't want to be butting into her business.

And honestly, she didn't really want to talk about her life story. It wasn't glamorous, and it wasn't stuff she was proud of. Especially next to Keene, who had always been handsome and popular. He had grown into a fine man, one she couldn't believe wasn't married, but as far as she knew, no one had snagged him yet. Ladies were trying, she was sure.

Not her. Working two jobs and taking care of her family didn't leave time for anything else, and she didn't trust herself not to make a huge mistake again.

She'd asked the question about more men from the church, or anyone, coming, just because she knew if there were more people, it would seem less like Keene doing her a favor and more like the church was actually helping. If it was just him, her stupid heart was going to start to think that there was something special about him. She was sure of it.

She didn't used to be like that. But since her divorce and the emotional scars she carried from that, she was starved for affection. Attention. Just...anything.

A touch, a kiss, a compliment. It had been so long since someone looked at her and saw anything but an exhausted mom of three children struggling to make it.

Poor. Stupid. Never going to amount to anything.

And still, deep in her heart, under all of the mistakes and the realization that her life was going in a completely different direction than the one she had intended, under the guilt and embarrassment, there was still a woman who just longed to be loved.

God loves you.

She knew that. Even if she hadn't been in church in a long time.

Still, it was hard to feel God's love. Hard not to long for a physical touch. A caress. A soft word. Someone who looked at her and actually saw her, not her circumstances, and maybe they could even overlook her mistakes.

"I didn't mean to pry," Keene finally said, and she realized she'd never answered his question about the three kids.

There she was, spinning off into daydreams. A man like Keene had a tendency to make a woman like her want things that were impossible.

"That's right. Three. Two girls and a boy. Plus, my mom lives here as well."

She wasn't trying to impress him. There was no point. She didn't even like what she saw when she looked at herself—she'd not lived up to her potential. Not even a little. Keene certainly wouldn't see anything she didn't.

"The pastor has done some rough estimates to get the amount of lumber and materials he would need, but he didn't mark anything, like where the posts would go or anything," she said. Although, he could see it for himself that there were just steps outside the door and nothing on the ground had been marked in any way.

"That's fine. I'll be better off doing it myself anyway. That way if it's done wrong, at least it's done wrong according to my specs."

She laughed a little, having never heard that before. "I highly doubt that you'll do it wrong."

Back in school, Keene was the kind of guy who did everything well. From the sports he played, to the classes he took, to going to nationals with the Parliamentary Procedure team. It had been a big deal at their small school.

She hadn't been too shabby herself, having been chosen out of all of the kids in school to paint a mural in the cafeteria. Which, as far as she knew, was still there. She'd also played the flute and piccolo in the band and had gone to states for that although she hadn't chaired.

But that was then, and all the accomplishments of fifteen years ago didn't mean anything since she hadn't really accomplished anything worth noting since she'd graduated from high school. She considered her three children a more than worthwhile accomplishment, but her biggest fear was that she would let them down.

"Do you mind if I take measurements while I'm here and then back my pickup around and unhook that trailer as close as I can? I'm not going to take the time to unload it. Since I don't need the trailer, I can leave it here. Unless you have a problem with that?"

"No. Please, do whatever you need. My mom will be home from shopping soon, and I'm going to start supper. You're welcome to stay and eat if you'd like."

He had put his head down and moved as though he were going to start walking away, but her invitation froze him.

He tilted his head and looked at her, almost as though he couldn't believe she had invited him to stay.

"I appreciate the invitation. Might take you up on it some other time when I'm working and don't want to leave to eat. But tonight, I have...plans."

She got the impression again that it wasn't just farm work that he needed to do. But that wasn't her business either though it made something funny wiggle in her chest. Uncomfortable.

"Anytime you're here, you're welcome to eat when we are. I'll make sure to say something."

He stared at her, the wind rustling the corn leaves, blowing strands of hair across her face. She reached out, pushing them back, and his eyes glanced at her hand before he jerked his head.

"I appreciate that." He pulled a measuring tape out of his pocket. "I'll just be a few minutes. You don't need to babysit me. Then I'll park the trailer and get out of your hair."

He turned around and walked toward the edge of the trailer, and she did not allow herself to watch him like she wanted to do for some weird reason.

Instead, she tried to think about what she was going to have for supper, what she needed to do with her children before she left for work, and tried to steel her heart against any soft feelings for the handsome neighbor who was only doing a good deed for Christmas.

Chapter 3

"This broccoli is overcooked," Lacey said, using her fork to poke delicately at the bright green vegetable on her plate.

Keene jerked his head, unwilling to agree with her because it would be a lie. In his opinion, it was undercooked. Vegetables shouldn't still be crunchy when he went to eat them.

Although, his gram had hammered into his head that he should eat his vegetables his entire childhood, so he was crunching on it dutifully. Even if he wasn't too happy about it.

Lacey put up her fingers, waving them in the air. "Waiter. Excuse me."

Her voice was cultured and sweet although Keene heard tones of irritation. Or maybe that was just his imagination. Since the tones had been there all night.

"Yes, ma'am?" the waiter said, coming to their table with a white towel over his arm, his gloves perfect, his black-and-white uniform crisp.

"My salmon is undercooked. And the broccoli is overdone. Please take my meal back to the kitchen and tell them I want each person responsible for this to try it and note their mistakes. I'm sure they'll do a better job next time." She looked down her nose, her lips pursed, her displeasure obvious even though her expression was pleasant and her tone level. "My father highly recommended your kitchen, but I can't say that I agree with him."

Her brows twitched ever so slightly, and her lips flattened just a fraction more before she closed her eyes and moved her head back. She opened them and gave Keene a sweet smile.

"Darling. Before the waiter leaves, is there anything about your meal that you need to discuss with him?"

Somehow, Keene got the idea that he was supposed to complain as well. But even though he would prefer his broccoli to be cooked a little more, and his steak a little less, there wasn't anything about it that he couldn't get down, and the taste was truly incomparable. He couldn't even grill a steak that tasted that good on his own. And that was saying something since he considered himself something of a guru when it came to grilling.

"No, thank you. This is the most delicious meal I've had in a long time. It's even better because I didn't have to cook it myself. Give my compliments to the chef and staff, please." He nodded his head at the waiter, who seemed to be struggling to keep the relieved and grateful look off his face. He pinched his lips together, and the severe, stern look reappeared.

"Thank you, sir. I will." He bowed just slightly, picking up Lacey's plate. "I'll be back with a fresh meal, cooked to your specifications, ma'am. Is there anything else I can get you while you're waiting?"

"I would like fresh lemon for my water please. This one tasted like it had been in the refrigerator for three days."

"My pleasure, ma'am. Anything else?"

Lacey sniffed and shook her head. The waiter bowed once more and hurried away.

Lacey sighed, a gentle sigh that still somehow screamed that she was put out. "If you keep eating, you're going to be done before my food even arrives."

Keene stopped with the fork halfway to his mouth. He wanted to say that if he quit eating, his food would be cold before her food came back out and he wasn't the one who wasn't happy with his meal and sent it back. But he supposed that would be impolite and inconsiderate.

And also selfish.

Even if he felt like maybe Lacey was being a little bit dramatic and a lot picky, it was still selfish of him to want to eat while his food was hot instead of waiting so they could eat together.

"You're right. I'm sorry." He set his fork down and tried not to moan in frustration. He was starved. Typically, he ate at five or so in the evening. Waiting until eight had been hard enough. Now, having his warm and almost perfectly cooked steak in front of him and to not be able to eat it but to sit here and let it get cold was almost sacrilege.

But he wasn't going to die. He certainly wasn't going to starve to death, and he didn't want to be rude—even if he had already decided that Lacey and he would not be having another date.

If she complained through their date, she'd complain through their relationship, and he didn't even want to think about marriage to such a person.

Nothing he would do would ever be right, and it would be frustrating for both of them to be in a marriage like that.

Other than complaining, Lacey hadn't been a bad date, but he wasn't interested in dating just for the sake of dating. For the sake of having a warm body beside him. It seemed like a waste of time.

The scent of his steak drifted up to his nose, and his stomach growled loudly.

Lacey's eyes grew big, horrified, and he almost apologized. But while he'd wait for her food to come out before he'd eat, he wasn't going to apologize for being hungry since that was technically her fault anyway.

She lifted her nose and looked away.

He racked his brain for something to talk about. He'd already tried talking about the farm, which she hadn't been interested in. He tried to discuss construction, which she hadn't known anything about, and she had started topics about the latest Hollywood movies and several different TV shows which had been popular.

He'd drawn blanks on both of those subjects since he knew nothing about Hollywood and didn't even own a TV.

"Does Linglestown have a Christmas parade?" he asked, hoping that maybe this would be a subject they could converse on without awkward pauses and one of them shrugging their shoulders. Disinterested.

"It does." She wrinkled her nose. "Don't you just hate those? They snarl up traffic, you can't get anywhere, and people let their kids run around everywhere. Honest-to-goodness, I almost hit a child who ran out in the street right in front of me for a piece of candy. It was terrible. I had to go home and lie down, I was so upset." She sighed, one hand coming up and adjusting one of the sparkling earrings in her ear.

"Yeah. Poor kid. Bet he was scared too."

"I don't think so. The little hellion thought it was hilarious, and he was still laughing when I drove away. Shaking."

"Kid must have more courage than brains, then. He's not gonna win in a showdown against a car. Even if it is a fancy sports thing." When he'd picked her up in his pickup, there'd been a low-slung, bright yellow sports car sitting in her driveway. The windows had been tinted, and it looked expensive. He honestly wasn't even sure what kind of car it was.

He spent most of his free time reading up on chicken diseases and researching farm equipment.

He was thankful she hadn't suggested they take her car. He would have felt like he needed a crane to get out of it, it was so low to the ground. Although, he had to admit it would probably be fun to drive.

"So you don't typically attend the parade?" he asked, figuring he knew what her answer would be but not able to think of another question that would spur conversation.

"Don't be silly. That's for people who have little kids, and I don't. Thankfully. Children are just a drain on a woman, and they contribute to world hunger. I'm doing my part to help keep the world from being overpopulated and to protect our precious Earth from climate change." Her smile indicated that she felt very self-righteous and important for her contribution to the greater good of the world.

Keene figured they probably had different ideas about a lot of things, population control and climate change being just two of them. He was perfectly okay with differing opinions—good people could and did disagree, but her self-righteous tone indicated she felt she was taking the moral high road, which annoyed him. Unless she could support her position with chapter and verse, it was just an opinion and certainly not a moral one.

She'd hit on one of his pet peeves. Remembering that everyone needed grace—himself most of all—he tried again. "I heard we're supposed to get a snowstorm, possibly at the end of the week if things line up right. That's always fun." He loved snow, loved blizzards, and understood that while not everyone did, and they were major pains for some people, it didn't mean that he couldn't still enjoy them.

It seemed like nowadays, if someone was offended, it meant that everyone had to stop enjoying whatever it was that offended them. Keene wasn't sure he understood the logic behind that. He just walked away from things that bothered him or ignored them. But he would never dream of making everyone else stop doing what they enjoyed just because he didn't.

Maybe he was thinking wrong, but he should have picked a better subject than a snowstorm because Lacey wrinkled up her nose delicately.

"I hate snow. Hate the cold. I really hate the wind. Do you know how difficult it is to get your hair to look just right, and then you step out and the wind destroys it within a matter of seconds. It's terrible. And after the snow comes the mud. Don't even get me started on that."

Okay. He wouldn't. "I like sunshiny days too." There. That should keep her from complaining about mud.

"Unless it's too hot. Then the sun is a pain as well. Give me some climate control and fluorescent lights. I want to determine what temperature it is and how much wind I feel. I could live indoors forever." She shivered. "No bugs either. Or rodents, Heaven forbid."

Keene thought about the mouse that he'd had on the egg belt just that evening. He'd killed it with his hand. Not necessarily because he'd wanted to, but because rodents spread diseases, and he didn't want to lose a flock of twenty thousand chickens just because he didn't care to kill things.

Mice were better than rats, though.

Yeah. Pretty sure Lacey wasn't gonna want to talk about that.

They sat in silence for a while, with Keene thinking since he was the man, he should be coming up with a subject to talk about, but kind of wishing that Lacey could at least think of something since everything he'd tried, she'd pretty much shot down.

It'd be different if he came up with a subject and she helped him out. But it was almost like she was making it as difficult as possible for them to converse.

Or maybe her opinions just rubbed him the wrong way.

Still, she was Miss Dorothy's granddaughter and a very nice person, from what he understood from Miss Dorothy, so he kept trying to look beyond the complaints that he disagreed with to the wonderful person beneath.

"I've heard you work for a lot of charities. With your dad being the mayor, you have a lot of opportunity to do good." He was a big believer in giving back to the world. Although, a man had to make a living too. And first. The Bible was pretty clear that a man wasn't a good man if he didn't provide for his household first.

"I have some charities that I just love. Charity galas and banquets are so much fun. There is just nothing better than the crystal lights, the sparkling clothes, and rubbing shoulders with people who have money and know how to behave." She spoke in kind of a dreamy voice, like she truly did enjoy it, and Keene tried hard not to pull at the neck of his button-down. Just the idea of a black-tie affair made him feel a little strangled.

It felt like forever until the waiter finally brought Lacey's food back out. A man in a white outfit, wearing a hairnet, walked beside the waiter and carried Lacey's plate.

"Ma'am?" the waiter said, his face serious but concerned, his voice giving away his nervousness. "This is our head chef and kitchen manager, Leonard. He received your instructions and prepared your meal himself. He also wanted to bring it out and watch while you taste it, if that's okay with you, to make sure everything meets your standards."

Far from being embarrassed by the attention, Lacey gave a small smile and inclined her head as though she deserved it.

"Very well." She adjusted her fork as though it were in the way, but it wasn't, as the chef set her plate down in front of her.

Keene got the idea that she was enjoying the attention, and it made his stomach curl, and not in a good way.

Or maybe that was the one bite of steak he'd had settling.

After taking a delicate bite of her salmon, she closed her mouth and seemed to swish the food around a bit before swallowing and dabbing at her lips with her napkin. A small bit of pink lipstick came away as she set her napkin down.

"Much better. Apparently, whichever understudy cooked the salmon originally has a few more things to learn from the master."

"Thank you, ma'am," Leonard said, all but groveling. "And the broccoli?"

"Of course." Lacey lifted her fork and did the same thing with the broccoli.

Keene figured he didn't have to wait any longer but could dig back into his steak, which unfortunately was now cold. Still, it was food, and he was starving. He could probably have eaten one twice the size and maybe should have ordered a larger one. He wasn't used to the prices on the menu, though. It wasn't exactly that he couldn't afford it, he just couldn't bring himself to throw away that kind of money on food. The price of the larger steak would buy twenty-five pounds of hamburger.

By the time Lacey was done and the chef and the waiter left, he was putting the last bite of his steak in his mouth. He almost laughed to himself. He probably should have just eaten it, instead of waiting.

Chapter 4

As the waiter and chef walked away, Lacey looked at his plate. Her brows went up. Her mouth flattened.

"I'm not sure why you waited," she said, gently picking up her knife and cutting, yes, cutting, her broccoli.

"Yeah. It would have been better hot." His stomach twisted uncomfortably, and not because of her words. It felt like he'd eaten something rotten.

"I'm sorry I inconvenienced you." Her expression was anything but sorry, and he got the feeling she expected him to say he hadn't been inconvenienced.

"Not a problem." Despite having said this, his stomach had started rolling, truly feeling terrible, and it wasn't because of the way she was acting.

He was fine if someone had a bad meal and they wanted to complain about it. Although, his grandma had brought him up that he should be happy with what he had and be grateful without complaining. So the idea that complaining was a right was a little foreign to him. But considering the prices on the menu, if a person was paying that much for something, he'd want to get what he was paying for, but...it just still seemed like a complaint should be something extremely serious.

Regardless, he tried to eat his broccoli slower. Which really wasn't hard to do. It wasn't his favorite vegetable anyway, and cold, crunchy broccoli just really wasn't doing it for him.

At the same time, every time he swallowed it felt like a brick landing at the bottom of his ribs.

He tried to ignore it, but by the time he had the last piece of broccoli down, he was pretty sure he was going to have to excuse himself to use the restroom.

He managed to sit until Lacey put her fork and knife next to her plate. She had taken four bites of her salmon and eaten half a piece of broccoli.

"I'm stuffed. I just couldn't eat another bite."

It hardly seemed worth sending her food back to the kitchen if she was only going to eat a half of a piece of broccoli and four bites of salmon, but who was he to say anything?

"Mine was quite tasty too," he said, *even if it was cold*, but he added that last part only in his head.

His stomach rolled again, and his intestines cramped.

"I think I'm gonna have to find the restroom. I must have eaten something that didn't agree with me." As much as he hated to admit it. He'd never left a date early, but from the terrible way he was feeling, there was no getting around it.

He couldn't imagine the after-dinner conversation was going to be any more stimulating than the before-dinner conversation.

Her eyes widened, and he got the impression she didn't realize her mouth hung open. "You're leaving?"

"Not leaving the restaurant. Just leaving the table. Unless you want whatever's going to come out to come out here?" He shouldn't have said that last bit. He just didn't appreciate being questioned about whether or not he really needed to leave the table. Like he was two and couldn't really be sure whether he had to use the restroom or not.

"I'm sorry. I didn't mean to offend you," she said, sounding offended that he was offended.

The person who is the most offended is the most powerful person in the room.

Where had he heard that? He wasn't sure, but that seemed to be the way things were now, and Lacey seemed to have the principle down to a T.

It hadn't been the way he'd been raised, and it wasn't the way he would be acting now. Unfortunately, he was also raised to be careful of other people's feelings, which was tough to do when people insisted on being constantly offended.

He sighed. "Please, excuse me."

"Do you mind if I come along?" Lacey said, a little snippy, but at least she was still talking to him.

"Please." He was already standing, and he held his hand out for her.

He thought she might ignore it, but it felt like the polite thing to do.

To his surprise, she put her hand in his. It slipped in gently, almost delicately. Much softer than the other hand he'd held earlier today. Funny he would flash back to that as long, slender fingers slid through his and she gripped his hand.

He'd only meant to help her up, not hold her hand, but he wasn't going to split hairs when she didn't release his hand and he would have needed to make a scene to get his hand back.

He needed to get to the restroom. His gut felt like it was about to explode. Hurt. And rolled.

The steak had been good, but they'd had some kind of breaded seafood for an appetizer. Maybe that was it. Or maybe he was just coming down with a stomach flu.

He wasn't sure, but he did really hate the fact that he was leaving his date and going to the bathroom. At least she was coming with him.

"Do you think you're going to take very long?" Lacey asked, her head up, her stride sure, her face arrogantly lifted. She looked every inch a classy lady, if a little bit snobby too.

Keene couldn't fault her looks at all, couldn't fault much of anything about her other than the evening had held a lot of complaints.

"I hope not," he said as they walked through the almost empty country club restaurant. He had seen bathrooms by the door when they walked in, but Lacey seemed to know her way around and was leading him toward bathrooms in the back. He saw the sign for them and quickened his step. They would be getting there none too soon.

"Oh," Lacey said, her steps slowing, her hand pulling back on his.

And then he saw what she was looking at. The janitor had just hooked a chain across the men's restroom and was adjusting the sign that said "Closed for Cleaning."

They were too far away for him to yell across the room to stop her, but as the chain hooked and her eyes lifted, met his, he just had a second to recognize the September-sky-blue eyes from earlier in the afternoon before Shelby's face closed and she whirled, heading into the men's restroom.

"I can't believe it. She saw us coming and turned around and went into the bathroom anyway. How rude!" Lacey exclaimed.

"Looks like your bathroom isn't closed." Keene gritted his teeth. He could probably turn around and walk to the front of the restaurant, but...he felt like he was already pushing his luck. It was all he could do to walk upright and not be doubled over. Couldn't remember the last time he felt this terrible.

"If you're going to the front, I am too. Of course, I wouldn't stay here without you."

"I'm staying. She just walked in, and I'm sure she doesn't want to be in there with me; she'll come out." The idea of being sick in the restroom with a strange woman wasn't exactly high on his list of things he wanted to do, but he was almost at the point where he really didn't care.

"Wait for me when you get out."

"I will," he said absently. With as bad as he felt, it might take a bit. But he didn't go into all of that with Lacey, not wanting to face her disapproval or censure or offend her yet again. It seemed like every time he opened his mouth, he offended or upset her. It hadn't been a pleasant evening.

Lacey opened the restroom door and stepped inside, not looking back, while Keene grabbed the chain and unhooked it. He waited for the ladies' restroom door to clunk shut before he spoke, turning around at the same time and re-hooking the chain.

"Shelby? Sorry to bother you, but it's kind of an emergency." He walked around the corner and saw Shelby's body popping up, her face turning toward him, her eyes big.

This was the job that she was going to. The first one anyway since she said she'd worked until dinnertime. There must be another job since it wouldn't take all night and through the morning to clean the country club restaurant.

Still, he wasn't going to take the time to figure it out now. He needed to be where she was.

Chapter 5

"Keene? I'm cleaning," Shelby said, like he could have somehow missed the sign or the chain. Either one would be a stretch.

"I know. I'm sorry. I just... I'm having an emergency." He didn't want to get graphic or crude. But he also didn't have time to stand around and chat about it. He hoped his emphasis on "emergency" would be enough to convince her.

"You're sick! Goodness. You're as white as a sheet of paper." She rushed out of the stall, her eyes concerned, her mouth pursed. "Are you sure you're going to be okay?"

"I'm sure. Although, if I die, maybe you could make sure someone gets my pants up before a bunch of people come and look at me."

The concerned look didn't leave her face, but she snorted. "I'll do that. The dying man's last wish. How could I not?"

"Thanks. It's encouraging that you think I might actually die. Do I look that bad?" he mumbled as he walked by her, maybe a little embarrassed to be rushing to the bathroom but not really having any choice.

"You do. In fact, I'll stand here by the door, but I'm not leaving. You look awful."

"Thanks. I'll return the compliment after I feel a little better."

"Don't give me a compliment if it's not true," she said, and he thought her words sounded a little bitter. Like maybe she'd been lied to before.

"Burned by compliments?"

"I guess you could say that. My whole marriage was basically built on them. I was a stupid fool who was just desperate for attention...love."

She said "love" like it was a four-letter word. Which, come to think of it, it was. But when a guy had to use the bathroom as badly as he did, his brain didn't function quite as quickly as it normally might.

"That stinks," he said, somehow wishing that things had been different for her. He maybe understood a little of how it felt to long for

29

some kind words, a gentle touch. Someone to back him up and have fun with.

Another wave of pain and nausea blew that from his mind, though, and he almost forgot about her until she spoke.

"Should I go say something to the woman you were with?" she asked, and he realized he'd groaned.

Trying to get a hold of himself, he forced his voice to sound as normal as possible. "She knew I wasn't feeling well."

"Okay." Shelby didn't say anything more, and neither did he for a while.

Finally, he felt like he could get up and walk around without having to rush back to the stall, but he took his time, thankful when he came out that Shelby wasn't in sight. She must have been standing on the other side of the entranceway wall, giving him privacy but also being there in case he needed her.

He washed his hands and glanced at his reflection in the mirror, agreeing that Shelby was right. His face was extremely white, and he didn't look well at all. She hadn't been exaggerating.

He walked around, and she was right there, exactly where he'd expected her to be.

Maybe that would make some guys feel smothered, but he appreciated her giving him his privacy while still being close enough that she could help him if necessary. Or go get help.

"Better?" she asked, her head tilted, half smile, half grimace on her face. Like she was commiserating with him. "It sounded terrible."

"That's embarrassing," he said.

"I'm sorry. But I just couldn't walk away. I was afraid you might need something, and I wanted to be there in case you called for me."

"I appreciate it. I truly felt terrible. I still don't feel the greatest, but I think I can make it to my truck at least."

"The girl you were with told me to tell you she called a friend who was picking her up. And you didn't have to worry about taking her home."

He nodded. Partially relieved, partially irritated. If Lacey had been sick in the bathroom, he wouldn't have left her.

But maybe that was a man-woman thing, and he supposed he should be grateful that she figured he was a big boy and could take care of himself.

"Nobody has any loyalty anymore, do they?" he said, shaking his head and smiling at Shelby.

He was more embarrassed that his date had ditched him than he was about the noises he'd been making in the bathroom. At least the noises were natural.

Even if he hadn't been having the best time on his date, he wouldn't have just left.

"Maybe she was tired," Shelby said, her eyes seeming to search his face. "I can't imagine anyone would leave you voluntarily." Her mouth snapped shut, like she hadn't meant to say that, and then she kind of laughed, like it was a little joke.

He still wasn't feeling the greatest. Maybe he was just imagining things because it was almost like she was saying Lacey shouldn't have left.

"I don't think she thought I was a very good date. We didn't have a whole lot in common, and I think I irritated her."

"I can't imagine. Maybe she's not feeling well either but just didn't want to say. Did you guys eat something that was the same?"

"Some kind of breaded fish stuff as an appetizer. Although, I don't think she had a whole lot of it." She hadn't eaten much of anything all evening.

"That could do it. Fish is a common cause of food poisoning." Her eyes seemed to rove over him again as though looking to see if he'd lost any body parts. "You seemed fine earlier today when we spoke. I hope you didn't catch anything at my place."

"No. I'm sure I didn't although I don't know what it was. I haven't been that sick in a while, and I have a feeling it's not over. I guess I'm kind of glad I don't have to take Lacey home. I think I'll be spending the night not too far away from the bathroom."

"Is there someone there to make sure you're okay?" she asked. It was probably just the mother in her coming out. Not necessarily like she was hinting around about anything.

"Normally there would be, but I'm at the farm alone for a couple of weeks until Gram is recovered from her surgery. Probably at least until Christmas or after."

"Do you have someone you can call if you need them?"

He liked the fact that she was concerned and making sure he was okay but she wasn't jumping on the opportunity to give him her phone number. He would have felt a little bit weird about that—talking to someone for one day, and all of a sudden, they're throwing a number at you.

"I do. Thanks for checking." He glanced around, his eyes falling on the chain and the underside of the sign. "I'm sorry that you had to close the bathroom longer than normal, and I'm sorry to interrupt your work."

"Not a problem. It's not the first time it's happened if you can believe that. And it was pretty obvious that you needed it."

He felt like he should offer to take her home or something. But that would be dumb. She was working. He just...while he couldn't wait to get away from Lacey and had to rack his brain to try to think of things to say to her, he didn't want to leave Shelby. Wanted to ask how late she was working, and what her second job was, and whether she'd gotten any more sleep, and even apologize for waking her up in the first place.

"I don't want to keep interrupting your sleep by coming and working on your addition. I just realized that the time that suits me might not suit you. Maybe you can let me know." And then he was tempted to give her his number when he had just been thinking that he was glad she hadn't been throwing her number at him. Now he was trying to think of an excuse to get hers.

"Whenever you do, it is fine. You're donating your time, which is huge, especially this time of year. Plus, you're doing all of your regular work on the farm. By yourself. I couldn't ask you to cater to my schedule."

That was the kind of woman he was used to. That he wanted. One who was considerate of others rather than demanding that everything be done to her specifications.

He shouldn't be comparing Shelby and Lacey, but his date had been an unmitigated disaster.

"Plus, you obviously have a personal life as well. I'm just super thrilled that it might even be finished before Christmas. Although, I don't have any expectations in that direction, so no pressure." She grinned at him, and he found himself grinning back, feeling like a fool. Just standing there in the bathroom doorway, grinning at the janitor.

She just had that pull on him.

"All right, then." He almost asked when she was going to be there because he wanted his free time to match up when he might have the best shot of seeing her. But that would defeat the purpose of trying to be quiet so he didn't wake her up. "I guess I'll see you around."

"I guess so."

He moved by her, unhooking the chain. She was gone by the time he turned back around to hook it.

Just as well. He had never considered dating a woman with children before, and Shelby seemed especially burdened. With working two jobs and raising her kids, she probably didn't have time for a relationship anyway. He shouldn't even be thinking in that direction.

She needed help, not a man who was going to suck even more time from the limited amount that she had.

Chapter 6

"And my teacher said I could bring pictures in for show-and-tell if it was too big to take in." Grace, who, at five years old, had just started kindergarten this past fall, stood by the sink, helping Shelby rinse off lettuce for their salad.

"We'll have to make sure we get you some. We should be able to print those off with no problem. Your day is next Wednesday?" Shelby asked, trying to focus on her child and appreciate the limited amount of time she got to spend with her. She didn't want to waste it.

"Yep. There's twenty kids in my class, and we all get a day each month. That way, everything's fair," Grace said, as though quoting her teacher.

"I'm glad your teacher's making it fair, but sometimes life isn't fair."

She didn't know why she felt the need to always make a lesson out of everything. But maybe she would have appreciated it if someone had warned her that life wasn't fair. That it was hard. That she needed to make smart decisions because one stupid mistake could mess up her life forever, just...just she wished she would have had someone wise and caring, someone who cared enough to help her so that she wouldn't have wasted so much of her life doing stupid stuff.

Her mom had always been working, too. When Shelby had time to spend with her kids, she wanted it to count. She would have appreciated advice. Really.

Why hadn't her college counselor told her that an art history degree was basically worthless?

Why hadn't someone told her that men lie, and that if she suspected that he was lying before they were even married, it was a huge red flag. And instead of closing her eyes and looking the other way, she should have confronted him. Closing her eyes and looking the other way wasn't trust, it was stupidity.

Too late. Too late. Too late.

But not too late for Grace. That was why she felt like everything needed to be a lesson. So Grace didn't end up like she did.

"Now, I'm going to give you the knife, and you're going to cut these tomatoes in half. Be careful, okay?" She didn't want her kids to be as ignorantly dumb as she had been about working in the kitchen, either.

She had been able to open a box and open a can and boil water.

But that's about all she'd left the house knowing.

It wasn't really her mom's fault. Her mom had worked and hadn't had time.

Shelby worked too, but she would make the time. She wouldn't go out on weekends or on her off days. She'd be here for her kids.

"Mommy?" Haley walked in the kitchen, rubbing her eyes. It had been a long day for her since she had preschool on Mondays and Thursdays. Mondays were Shelby's hardest days as well, and that made them hard for everyone.

"Yes, dear?" she said, stopping and giving Haley her undivided attention. She didn't want her children to think she was too busy for them.

"Can I set the table?"

"Please. That would be such a big help!" she said, making sure that her face relaxed completely in a grin and didn't just smile a little. She met Haley's happy eyes and was thankful she had made the effort.

As she handed her the plates and helped her count out the spoons, her mom came around the corner.

"This guy's changed. I don't think he's ever going to learn to go on the potty, are you, Perry?"

"Of course he is. I've always heard boys are harder to train than girls." She hated that people sometimes compared her children. She also didn't want her kids to be told that they couldn't do something. She felt like they could do anything. And she wanted them to feel that too.

But she wasn't going to argue with her mom, and she was grateful that her mom had agreed to move in with them when Stephen had left.

"Well, he didn't do it all today. So maybe tomorrow. I put a pull-up on him so we don't have any more accidents before bed."

"Thank you so much, Mom." Even though it was kind of her mom's job, and her mom was better off living with them because it cut her housing expenses way down and made her disability stretch further, it was still a sacrifice since she never knew when her fibromyalgia was going to flare up.

Shelby lifted the pot of pasta from the stove, trying to ignore the ache in her back. The couch was lumpy, but that normally didn't bother her. She must have slept on it wrong this afternoon.

She poured the pasta into the colander in the sink and waited for the water to drain out, trying to remember where the bottle of pain pills was. She'd need one before she went to work tonight in order for her to be able to do all the cleaning needing to be done at the country club.

At the convenience store, she could probably get away with nothing. That job wasn't as physical.

Pounding outside reminded her that Keene had come as he'd promised. He'd been working since the middle of the afternoon, and though all the pounding had woken her up when he'd first gotten there, she'd been able to fall back asleep.

It had almost been comforting. The idea that someone was here, caring about her and taking care of them. Even if he had been sent by the church.

"Would you like to put the butter in, Haley?" she asked her daughter who had come into the kitchen and was standing with her little eyes glued on her mom.

Haley's lips turned up, and she nodded eagerly.

"You can unwrap this while I go get a chair for you to stand on. Just wait."

Haley took the butter and started looking for the edge of the wrapper while Shelby went the few steps to the eating area and grabbed a chair, picking it up and carrying it over to the stove.

She hadn't asked Keene how he was doing. She didn't have his number and hadn't seen him since they'd parted ways at the country club. She hadn't gone out to talk to him today, either. Mostly because she'd been fighting herself. Keene was a good man. Honest and upright, and the kind of man she'd love to be with.

But their differences had been in stark contrast and on blatant display on Friday evening.

He was at the country club as a guest. He had the kind of woman on his arm that he deserved to be married to. One with poise and class. One who knew which fork to use and used the restroom like normal people. She didn't clean it for normal people. She used it.

And there was Shelby, in her uniform, doing the lowliest of low jobs and hanging out just out of sight while Keene was sick in the bathroom she was supposed to clean.

It had brought home to her how far-fetched the idea of them ever being more than casual acquaintances and possibly surface friends was.

Not a chance.

Not to mention, the woman he'd been with was gorgeous and she didn't have children. Hadn't been married. Wasn't trying to pay off her husband's gambling debts. Wasn't living in a dump and working two jobs to make ends meet. Wasn't spending all of her spare time and energy trying to be a half-decent mom to her little children.

Wasn't wading through the rubble of her dreams and wondering how her life had come to this.

She wasn't necessarily upset with herself for dreaming. She was more upset with herself that she wanted to take the coward's way out and ignore him. But she'd promised that she would invite him in if they ate while he was there, so as she opened the jar of spaghetti sauce and handed it to Haley to pour in on top of the noodles, she said, "Once we get this stirred up, would you guys like to come over to the door with me and we'll see if Mr. Keene wants to come in and eat with us?"

The girls jumped up and down and said, "Yay!" And she smiled at their exuberance. All the while pushing aside the hope that he would say he'd already eaten and no thank you.

Haley was very careful in particular, especially for a four-year-old, and it took a little while for the spaghetti to get stirred. In the meantime, her mom put Perry in his booster seat and then said in a casual tone, "Would you like to go to the restroom and freshen up a little, Shelby?"

Shelby jerked her head around at her mom. She wasn't looking at her but was handing a cracker to Perry to keep him happy in his booster seat.

She looked back at the spaghetti, shaking her head. She didn't say anything because she didn't want her children to hear her saying she wasn't good enough for Keene, and the last thing she wanted was for her children to think that they might not be good enough. And it was a lie to say her thoughts weren't going in that direction.

If you don't want your children to say it, why are you allowing yourself to think it?

Right. That made sense.

Except, it was true. People looked at someone like her, who had basically failed at life so far, and they didn't know that she was determined to do better. That she would get out of the hole that she'd fallen into, or jumped into, or maybe a little of both.

"No. We're just gonna go ask him because if he is, we're ready to put it on the table." That was all she said to her mom and all that really needed to be said.

Although, as Haley jumped down from the chair and grabbed her hand and Grace fell into step beside her, she walked by her mom who looked up and met her eyes.

Her mom's look was reproachful. Maybe there was a little bit of pleading in it. Maybe pleading for the girl she used to be. Confident

and even a little cocky. She'd been smart and popular and full of potential when she graduated from high school.

Life had just beaten her down.

It was only a few steps to the back door, and she opened it to a
deepening night. That winter dark that seemed to last forever as the
days flowed toward the winter equinox.

"Hey." Keene looked up from where he was tamping down the dirt
around a post, a bag of ready-mix cement beside him and the hose
spread out over the yard. The day had been cool, and with the sun
down, it was downright chilly as Shelby stood in the door.

She noted he wasn't using gloves and only had a sweatshirt on.
"Aren't you cold?" came out of her mouth before she could remember
that she was supposed to be inviting him in to eat.

He grinned, looked down at his shirt, and shrugged. "No. When
I'm working, I don't like to have a lot of bulky stuff get in my way. You
get acclimated to the cold, and you don't even think about it."

"No gloves?"

"Some guys work in them pretty good, but I just don't." He lifted a
shoulder like he didn't know why, it just was.

"I made the salad," Haley said, staring at the man in front of her like
she had never seen a person before.

"Wow. I didn't realize someone as little as you could make a salad.
That's pretty good."

She beamed, and her little chest stuck out a bit more. "Mommy
taught me. I put extra onions in it because I love onions."

"I love onions too. They're pretty helpful when you have people
hanging around who you'd like to see go home."

Shelby grinned, but Haley just looked confused.

"That's because onions make your breath smell bad, silly," Grace
said, seeing the confusion on her sister's face and not waiting for her to
ask a question.

"I helped Mom make the spaghetti. Then we came out here to ask if you want to come in and eat with us. Mom said she promised you she'd ask. Mom always keeps her promises." Grace, at five, was a typical oldest child and took control of the situation.

"She does?" He met Grace's serious stare. "Not every kid has a mom who does that. Gotta make sure you appreciate her."

Grace didn't seem to either know what appreciate meant or know what to say to that because she just stared at Keene. Finally, she said, "Are you coming in?"

Keene's eyes went to Shelby's, his brows lifted even though she was standing there, which probably meant that she was okay with it.

"That's why we're here. To ask. Because we want you to join us." She didn't want him to think that she was just keeping a promise. Of course, that was part of it, well...maybe more of it than she wanted to admit. But it wasn't because she didn't want him. Wasn't because she didn't want to be around him because they weren't...they weren't equal.

Being around him made her feel less than. He almost rubbed it in. Making her have to stare in the face of the fact that she wasn't on the same footing as he was even though they'd pretty much started out equal in high school.

It made her depressed, not to mention it made her long for things that she couldn't have. Like a man who was a busy farmer and already worked hard but would give some of his valuable time to help someone he barely knew.

Long for things like that. Things like a man at the table, someone who valued her for her brains and ability and supported her, and it wasn't just her putting everything into a relationship and getting nothing in return except bills and a broken heart.

"You caught me at a good place to stop, and that smells pretty good coming out the door. Don't mind if I do."

Chapter 7

"Come on in. You can use this door and don't worry about your boots," Shelby said, stepping back as he leaned the tamper against the fence and walked over to the door.

"Mommy said we could take some pictures of what you're doing and I can take them in for show-and-tell," Grace said as Keene reached the steps.

"Did you get some with the footers in?" Keene asked her, jerking his head toward the posts that were sticking out of the ground.

"Mommy?" Grace's eyes went to Shelby.

"I can do that right now." She pulled her phone out of her pocket and walked back to the doorway, which was completely blocked by Keene, his broad shoulders filling it.

He stepped aside as she reached him, but his scent lingered. Manly and good, it smelled honest and right, and she tried not to be obvious about wanting to breathe it in.

It'd been a long time since she'd been around a man who smelled that good.

Even while he was working.

"What are those strings for?" Grace asked while Shelby was taking some pictures.

"I want to make sure everything's square. And I want to make sure I have everything measured correctly. One little mistake at the beginning can compound itself, until by the time I finish, I don't actually have a corner but more a suggestion to turn."

Shelby chuckled although Grace didn't seem to get the joke.

"When you start building something, you want to build it on a firm foundation. I guess it's a lot like your life. You want to make sure that everything you do is centered around God, or you get off-balance and off-kilter, and then you end up messed up somewhere. Same thing for a house or for a room. You want to make sure you get things centered on the right measurements so that everything that you do is square and upright. And that way, you end up with a really great finished product, instead of piecing and patching things together to try to make it look okay and get things to fit."

Shelby didn't say anything, and maybe she slammed the door shut a little harder than she needed to.

It was like he was preaching to her. She'd actually had a pretty good start in life, but as she'd gone about starting her adult life, she'd made poor choice after poor choice, and, yeah, maybe it wasn't her fault that her husband had gambling debts and he'd used her cards to pay for them, but there were some choices that she had made that had started her down that path.

She didn't need Keene in here smelling so good and reminding her of her stupidity.

"So if it's not right, you have to take it down and do it again?" Grace asked, showing an understanding that Shelby didn't think she would have.

"No. You just keep going with what you got, and you make it work the best you can. Sometimes you can patch it up pretty good, and it looks almost as good as if you did it right to begin with."

Shelby had started to turn, but as he spoke, she stopped and looked and found that he was staring at her.

He hadn't been preaching at her earlier, and if she were being honest, she knew it.

He wasn't preaching at her now. She didn't even think he was deliberately talking to her. He couldn't know how his words had affected her.

He had reminded her of grace. Reminded her that God's grace was sufficient.

That maybe she needed more of it than a lot of people, but there was an endless supply, and God was not stingy with it.

It was just herself she had to get over. And not be offended with other people who hadn't made the same mistakes she had.

"Come on in. You can wash your hands in the sink. We're ready to set food on the table. It's just spaghetti. I guess soup would have been a little nicer for you on a day like today."

She should have done that. She should have had a really good home-cooked meal, homemade bread along with the soup, something hot and hearty that would make him warm and ready to go back out and work in the cold.

Instead, she had spaghetti. Which Stephen always said wasn't a real meal. In fact, she'd never had it when he was home because all he would do was complain about how he hated it and how she should have cooked something more substantial.

Well, she just hadn't had time to cook soup, and she really hadn't had time to do homemade bread. Even if she could do that, which she'd never tried before, so she didn't know whether it was possible or not.

"Man, it smells even better in here than it does out there."

Keene was behind her, but she could hear her girls giggling and assumed he was probably looking at them. "Just ignore that growling. It's not a bear, it's my stomach. You ladies know how to wake it up."

"Maybe you have a bear in your belly," Haley said with a giggle in her voice.

"Maybe I do. Should I be worried about that?" His voice sounded truly perplexed, and Shelby had to beat her heart back down just because he was being so kind to her girls. That would make her heart stir anytime.

"As long as you can feed it, I don't think you have to worry about it," her mother said. "And by the way, I remember you from high school, but you probably don't remember me. I'm Cindy. Shelby's mother."

"I knew you in high school as Mrs. Henniger. It might be hard for me not to say that now, too."

"Cindy is better, but over the years, I've gotten used to Mrs. Henniger. Used to be it made me feel old. Now it sounds like me," she said, and it was funny that her mother had never said that to her before. But Shelby knew exactly what she was talking about. With the Mrs. in front of her name, it made her feel at least three decades older than what she actually was.

Although, when she'd worked both jobs and gotten home at dinnertime, she felt three decades older than what she was anyway, so it was a familiar feeling.

"I'm Keene. Just in case you didn't know. There are four boys in my family, and I'm the youngest, so I get pretty much everyone's name except for my own most of the time."

"Shelby's been talking about you some, so I knew your name. But you're right, all you boys look the same. It's easy to get confused."

"Shelby was talking about me, hmm," Keene mumbled as he stepped to the sink not two feet from where Shelby stood at the refrigerator bending over and getting the Parmesan cheese out.

"I like to warn my mother when I invite random strangers in for supper," she said, hoping that it seemed like she was just having a casual conversation with her mom and not discussing his merits as a husband. Or all the reasons why she couldn't marry him. Like marriage was something that had even come up. Yeah. She did not want him to know all the things she was saying about him.

"I see. I thought maybe you were regaling her with stories about the person who had gone running into the bathroom and was sick everywhere, interrupting your work and losing his date in the process. It was pretty unglamorous, even for me." He turned the water off and took the hand towel she had grabbed from the handle of the refrigerator where it usually hung and began drying his hands.

Funny the way their minds had gone completely different directions.

She'd been worried her mother was going to say what she actually had been talking about, and the thing that was stuck in his mind was that he thought he didn't look good.

"I think that spoke a lot more poorly about your date than it did about you. All of it. After all, it's not exactly your fault that you ate something that didn't agree with you. And you didn't make a mess everywhere. I cleaned the bathroom, remember? I know exactly what it looked like when you left. Which was no different than it did before you walked in."

Maybe she shouldn't talk about those things. They seemed like something that someone in polite society would avoid, but it was the truth, and there didn't seem to be any point in avoiding the truth, especially if it could make someone feel better. She didn't want him thinking that she had gone around, or would go around, talking about him being sick and possibly making fun of him for it. The idea hadn't even occurred to her although she supposed that there would be people who would consider doing that.

"Good to hear you weren't entertaining your mother with those stories anyway." He handed the towel back to her.

"I wouldn't entertain anyone with a story like that. It would be rude and unkind. I've made a lot of mistakes in my life, and I've got a lot of faults I need to work on, but that kind of rudeness and that kind of unkindness are usually things I don't have trouble with. No one's going to hear about what happened in that bathroom unless you tell them."

Maybe she was too serious. Maybe she was too determined that just because not all of her life had turned out the way she wanted it to didn't mean there weren't parts of her that were halfway decent. Even good maybe. That she wasn't a total heaping pile of messiness.

"I'm sorry. I didn't realize that me assuming that you probably told people about what happened made it seem like I thought you were unkind. It was a funny story, and I'll probably tell it myself. Once enough time has gone by that people won't be able to figure out who my date was. Because I guess I'm kind of in your camp. I wouldn't have left her if our situations had been reversed. But, to be honest, anyone who would leave wouldn't be someone I would want to have a second date with anyway. Not that I was thinking along those lines before that happened."

Shelby wasn't sure what to say about that. She'd been admiring his date although she didn't know her, thinking how classy and regal she was.

"You two looked good together," was all she could think of to say.

"I shouldn't have said that about her, but I guess you knew what she did, you just didn't know how I felt about it. Now you do."

"And I'm impressed because I would have been angry." She would be boiling mad if she had gone into the restroom sick and her date had left without caring whether or not she was okay. "Did she ever text or call to see how you were?"

"Not to see how I was."

Just the way he said that made it seem like maybe she texted him for something else. Despite her curiosity, Shelby figured it wasn't any of her business and clamped her mouth closed around the question she wanted to ask.

He opened his mouth, then closed it again. As though he was going to say more and then thought better of it.

It wasn't like they were even friends.

She hung the towel while he turned to the table.

"Help me out here, girls. Where should I sit? I don't want to accidentally sit in your mother's seat."

"She sat in my seat once, and I just sat in her lap," Haley said, and Shelby wanted to sink through the floor.

"I promise you, if you sit in my seat, I won't sit in your lap. I'm trying to quit."

Keene's eyes were dancing as he looked up, but he seemed like he was trying to keep a grin from taking over his face. "Me too."

Shelby didn't try to not laugh at that.

He looked back at the table and then said casually, "I've got a lot of bad habits I'm working on, and that one's really not at the top of the list anyway. So I can't guarantee if you sit in my seat, I won't end up sitting in your lap. Just warning you."

He glanced at Shelby but then looked back around the table at the girls, who giggled.

"You can sit on my lap!" Haley said, patting her legs like he might actually do it.

"I was thinking I would sit on your grandmother's lap. Hers looks like the most comfortable one, and I think she'd feed me too. The rest of you, you might let me sit on your lap, but I'm betting you won't let me eat your food."

"I'll share. We'll divide everything equally, although, I don't like hot pepper flakes on mine, so if you like it on yours, we'll have to divide our spaghetti first before Mom puts hot pepper flakes on it." Grace sounded quite serious.

"Your mom likes hot pepper flakes?"

"She says they build character. But I don't know what that means," Grace added.

"Character, huh?" he said with a lifted brow.

"We all have our little habits that we justify with religious reasons, ones that sound good but are completely inaccurate."

"In other words, you somehow twist the Bible to say that it's virtuous to eat food that burns your mouth and makes you miserable?"

"Also food that's healthy."

"So...you cook spaghetti and put hot pepper flakes on it and convince yourself you're eating health food? That's new. I like it. Creative."

"I also have salad. It's mostly lettuce, and I'll convince myself I'm only putting one serving of dressing on when I know I'm probably dowsing it with at least five."

"It's pretty much the only way a person can eat lettuce. Doused. And then preferably set on fire."

"You're not a rabbit?"

"Nope. Not a cannibal."

Her mother laughed at that along with her, but the kids missed the humor.

"I'm going to assume one of these two chairs is yours." He indicated the two empty chairs at the table while she set the salad dressing and the cheese on.

"Yeah. It doesn't matter. Whichever one you don't take."

"Mom usually sits here," Grace said, putting an end to that mystery.

"I see." Keene waited for her to start toward her chair, and then he started toward the same one. She thought maybe he really was going to sit on her lap just to be goofy, and she wasn't sure exactly how she was going to handle that, but he didn't.

Instead, he pulled her chair out for her.

"Ma'am," he said.

"Oh." Shelby put a hand to her chest. She certainly wasn't expecting that. She didn't know what to say. He flustered her.

Chapter 8

Keene had done something unexpected, something extremely nice and unexpected, and Shelby's first instinct was to make a joke, something about putting on royal airs in a dumpy trailer, but she didn't want to call attention to all of her deficits. Like they weren't already on display.

So she simply said, "Thank you." And sat down.

"You're welcome," he murmured as he left the back of her chair and went to sit down in the one that was left.

She liked that he didn't reach for the food but waited, and it made her think that he was used to saying grace before he began to eat. Of course. He was there from the church. It would make sense that he would do so.

Although, she'd been surprised over the years by the number of people who went to church but one would only know it by seeing their car in the lot on Sunday morning and not by watching how they lived the rest of the week.

Maybe that was part of the reason she hadn't made a superhuman effort to go even when she wasn't working.

There was no doubt Christians were supposed to be living a different kind of life, but there also was no doubt that most of them weren't.

She fit in the second category, and it wasn't necessarily something she was proud of.

Staying out of church seemed to assuage her guilt a little and was also easier than going and knowing she needed to change and putting the hard work in to do so.

Although, since Stephen had walked out, she'd gotten better. And not because she wanted people to look at her and see someone better but because the more her children looked at her and the more her relationship deepened with them, the more she saw the parallels between her relationship with her children and God's relationship with her.

She loved it when her children did right. Didn't fight. Chose to do something hard because they knew it would make her happy.

How much more it must make God happy to see her choosing to do right not because it made her look good but because she wanted to please Him.

Funny how children opened her eyes and gave a different perspective to everything.

"Keene, would you like to say the blessing?" she asked, not sure if she might be putting him on the spot, but he didn't seem the slightest bit alarmed at her question. Quite the contrary, his lips lifted up, and he nodded easily.

"Of course." He looked around the table at the faces of the children looking expectantly at him, and then he met her eyes once more. "Let's pray." He bowed his head without waiting for her reaction and began to speak to the Lord.

His prayer was simple, his words plain, the blessing asked like someone who expected an answer. His amen was said low, and her children repeated it along with herself.

Hearing his prayer, feeling like it was sincere and easy and natural for him to talk to the Lord, something he did on a regular basis, made her subdued as the table came alive with her children chattering, Perry talking gibberish, and Grace and Haley interpreting for Keene while Keene expressed admiration at how they could understand the convoluted words that were coming out of his mouth.

His respectfulness to her mother, his consideration as he passed things to her before he took any himself. All of that combined to make her feel guilty and bad for settling for someone like Stephen.

Surely Keene wasn't the only man in the world like this. Surely there were other men who were gracious and kind. Christians in more than just name. Funny with children, respectful and considerate.

Surely there were men like that in the world.

Figures, when she was obviously not a good catch for him, this is when she found one.

Maybe if she hadn't had children, if she hadn't ended up where she was, maybe she wouldn't have appreciated a man like Keene.

"Which one of you made the garlic bread?" Keene asked after Grace and Haley had told him all about how they'd made the salad and the spaghetti and there was a lull in the conversation which Perry wasn't filling with his gibberish.

"Mom made that," Grace said. "Mom helps us too. When she doesn't have to work, she makes better meals. And we get to help her."

"I see. Your mom's a good cook if this garlic bread is any indication," Keene said, and Shelby forced a smile. Of all the things he'd said at the table so far, that seemed like the most insincere. Like he was complimenting her for the sake of buttering her up or using flattering words, and they struck her wrong.

But who was she to judge? She didn't know.

Her smile became real, and she looked him in the eye. "Thanks. The key to good garlic bread is lots of butter."

"And a crispy crust," Keene added just before he bit into the bread. "This has both. Which makes it delicious."

It surprised her when he stayed and helped her clean up the table, carrying plates and bowls out while she wiped off the kids and wiped the table and her mom put food away.

The kids chattered around them, and it felt homey and comfortable, and she almost forgot he had to go back out to work.

"Thanks a lot for supper. I'll probably work for another hour or two if you don't mind leaving the floodlights in the back on. With that storm coming, I was kind of hoping I would get it all closed in. But I'm guessing I won't. It's supposed to start snowing this weekend."

"I know. If there's something I can do to help—"

"No." His word came out a little more harshly than anything he'd said, and it made her eyes jerk up.

His face softened.

"I'm sorry. You already work two jobs. You have a family to take care of. You look exhausted, and I'm guessing from the way you're walking a little hunched forward, your back hurts. If you have a few minutes before you have to go to work, take it easy. You don't have to come out and help me. In fact, I won't let you."

She bristled a little at those last words. It wasn't up to him to *allow* her to do anything, but he was saying it because he cared about her. Because he wanted to take care of her. Wanted to be considerate. How could she get offended over that? So she forced her ruffled feathers to smooth down and smiled at him.

"Thank you. Thank you very much. I...I appreciate..." She couldn't even articulate what she appreciated. Him being able to see that her back hurt? Or just him knowing that she was almost reaching her limit of everything that she could do and she shouldn't have offered to help when she probably couldn't?

He grinned. "It's okay. I'm keeping tabs. Don't thank me. I'll get it out of you later. In food. I'm kind of curious about those really good meals that Mom makes when she doesn't have to work," he said, quoting one of the kids from supper.

"Hopefully, you'll find out about it. Once the storm moves through and I have a day off, I'll plan on making something good. Do you have any preferences?"

"I want it to be dead when it hits the table. It can still be bloody, but it has to be dead. That's all I ask."

She laughed. "Got it."

They shared a smile, and he seemed to hesitate for just a moment before he turned around and left, walking out the back door and closing it carefully behind him and chattering with the girls until he disappeared.

"That man is a good catch," her mother said before the door had barely shut.

"Shhh!" Shelby hissed, looking around and seeing that the girls had gone to the window and climbed up on the couch where they could watch him working while they hung over the back of it.

Perry was trying to climb up and join them although he was a little slower since he wasn't quite as dexterous.

"Do you want them to hear you? The next time we're sitting at the table, that's what he's going to hear."

"So? There's nothing wrong with them saying that. It's true. The man's a catch. And you're an idiot for not going to the bathroom and at least combing your hair."

Her mother shook her head as she snapped the lid on top of the leftover spaghetti and opened the refrigerator door.

"Mother. Look at me. A man like that isn't interested in a woman like I am right now."

"But you're not going to be that woman forever. And you haven't been that woman all your life. And plus, underneath this," her mother said, straightening and shutting the refrigerator door, throwing a hand out and indicating the kitchen, the dumpy trailer, and the fact that she had three children and no husband and had to work two jobs in order to pay her bills, "underneath all of this, it's really about your character. The person you are. It's not about your environment."

"Mom, we both know that is in an ideal world. But men don't look at a woman and go, 'oh, I want to marry her because she has character.' They look at her, and they want to like what they see. They don't want to see a messed-up mom with three kids, who screwed up all of her potential, and made stupid choices, and will be paying for it for the rest of her life. You know that."

She wanted to believe what her mom was saying. And she did. That was the way *God* looked at people. Most of the time, she knew that and pretty much believed it. Although, sometimes she wondered if she hadn't screwed up so badly that even God wanted nothing to do with her.

And if she doubted whether or not God loved her, she certainly couldn't believe that there would be a man who could look past all of what she was and love her too.

"When you find the right man, that's what he'll see. You."

"There are a billion people in the world, Mom. The chances of me finding the 'right' man are pretty slim." She used her hands to put finger quotes around right before she wrung out the dishcloth and stretched it out on the sink.

"Maybe it's your attitude that needs work. Maybe God can't have the right man come along before you're ready for him. Because obviously you're not."

Her mother shuffled away, going to the couch and sitting down with her three children.

A glance at the clock confirmed that she didn't have time to go and cuddle with her kids; she needed to get ready. They'd lingered too long over supper although it had been fun.

Hmm, maybe her mom was right. Maybe it was her own attitude that stunk.

You know it is.

God wanted her to focus on the things that were pure and good and just and beautiful. He didn't want her to focus on all the bad things. When she thought about others and also when she thought about herself.

Thing was, she had struggled with pride and conceit in high school. She'd been smart and things had come easily, she'd been popular, and she'd given herself all the credit for everything good that had happened to her.

When, looking back, she hadn't really been lifting a finger to do much of anything. She certainly hadn't done anything to become smart, and she'd probably sacrificed more character than she wanted to admit in order to be popular. When she'd actually gotten out of high school and it had been time for her to start making her own decisions, that's when things went downhill. And it was all because of her.

But she was changing, and she would continue to change. Herself and her circumstances. And part of that was working to pay off her husband's debts.

She turned the light out over the sink and started walking to the hall closet where she kept her clothes.

First things first.

Get out of the hole she was in, and then maybe God would bring a man like Keene into her life when she had become someone who would interest a man like that. A woman who would interest a man like Keene.

Chapter 9

That Friday evening, Keene found himself in his pickup with the wrong woman beside him again.

He'd gotten a lot accomplished on the addition on Shelby's trailer working three of the five nights that week.

But Friday was the annual Prairie Rose school district Christmas program. The school was small enough that the elementary school and high school had their program on the same evening, and even though Keene didn't have any children of his own, he always went to support his nieces and nephews and also his neighbor, Bridget, who was now married to Shawn, and their three girls.

It was a fun time, and he always enjoyed being there.

He'd never minded going by himself either or with his brothers. Which is what they usually did. But despite the fact that Lacey had left him in the bathroom, she'd texted him the next day and hadn't asked how he was but had asked him to accompany her to the school performance Friday night. She'd mentioned her grandmother, Dorothy, and how she had suggested that since Keene was from Prairie Rose, he would be a good person to take her.

She'd mentioned that she had some kind of award to give out to the principal of the school, acting in place of her dad, the mayor of Linglestown, since he couldn't make it. She'd wanted to have a date, and she'd mentioned that she had turned several people down because she had been going on a date with him and expected to go with him Friday night.

It had been a lengthy text, one he hadn't wanted to read.

They didn't have anything in common, and he hadn't had a very good time on their first date. But that was no reason to dismiss someone out of hand. Especially since she declined other people because she'd been thinking she would go with him. Maybe it was that, or maybe it was her mentioning Miss Dorothy from church, who had been so eager for him to meet and like her granddaughter.

If she had called him, he probably would have declined, but sometimes subtext could get jumbled in a text, and he didn't want to hurt her feelings or offend her.

Regardless, he wasn't working on the addition although he had the material for the roof and the siding sitting on the trailer in the yard beside it.

"You're awfully quiet this evening."

Lacey hadn't said a word about their last date, which he considered a disaster. Any time he didn't take the girl home but was puking in the bathroom instead, he figured it probably hadn't turned out well for anyone.

"I guess I was thinking about what I want to talk to you about and trying to figure out how to say it without being clumsy."

She laughed, and it was a sweet sound. Maybe she had some growing up to do the same as he did, but maybe she'd make some lucky guy an awesome girlfriend and eventual wife. Some guy that wasn't him. Some guy that liked the things she did and didn't have to run to the bathroom in the middle of their date.

"Don't worry about that. Men are clumsy. And dumb. No offense, of course. And they typically don't say anything with finesse, without coaching." She sighed. "And they need a lot of coaching."

"Yeah. So...I don't want you to turn anyone else down because of me." He felt like he jumped into that a little fast, but he hadn't been able to find a way to lead into it gracefully and wanted to get it said.

"What?" she asked, her head snapping to his, her brows drawn.

"Well, I know you don't really like me since I'm kinda clumsy and inept, and I'm always gonna be a farmer and not very comfortable with the classy places you are. So, I didn't want you to feel like you had to keep taking pity on me."

So that might have been laying it on a little thick, but she seemed to be offended that he might not want to go out with her again. Everything he said was true. He wasn't right for her, for all of those reasons. He just didn't think they were bad reasons. Like she did.

"I see. You can learn to be better. All of us were born in Iowa, but we don't have to act like it."

"Actually, I love my state. I'm proud to be an Iowan. Proud to be a farmer too. But I get that in your circles, that's not something that people look at and admire. And I don't want you to be with someone who you're not proud to be with."

She was silent for a while as he pulled into the school. The parking lot was packed. It was the most popular night of the school year except for maybe the spring program. But there was just something about Christmas, and kids, and an evening full of festivities with friends and neighbors that drew people.

"Do you want me to let you off at the door? It's pretty cold out."

"Yes. I need to be backstage, but I'll wait for you at the door so we can find a seat together. Because once I hand out my award, I'll be back to sit with you."

He jerked his head and pulled up to the sidewalk so she could step out without having to walk on the blacktop at all.

She didn't say anything more but climbed out and hurried inside.

He drove to the back of the lot, figuring that moms with little babies and small children and grandparents could have the closer spots and he'd park his big truck somewhere out of the way. Since he was young and healthy, he could walk.

He reached the back row and found a spot that would work. Another car was coming the other way, but it didn't have its turn signal on, so he pulled into the open spot, assuming it would go by.

Instead, it pulled in right beside him.

He should have let it go first, but he hadn't been expecting it to park. Not that it mattered. There was plenty of time. At least fifteen minutes before everything started.

He got out, glancing casually at the car just in case there was a child or package that he could help carry, but he stopped and waited when he saw that it was Shelby.

"Seems like you just can't get away from me. I'm at your house all week long, now you run into me here."

"Well, to be clear, I didn't run into you, but that's more the grace of God than any skill of driving on my part."

She did have one front tire on the yellow line that separated their two parking places, and he figured she wasn't being falsely modest.

"Everybody has their abilities, I guess."

"Some of us are still searching for ours," she said, grabbing her purse out of the back of her car and slamming the door shut. Her car beeped twice as she locked it and walked to him.

"You don't have children, or did I miss that?" she asked as she stopped in front of him.

"I have nieces and nephews, and maybe you weren't around when your kids and I were talking about this, but Grace asked me if I was coming. She said she had a small part. I told her I wouldn't miss it."

"I forgot about your nieces and nephews."

"I take it you must have let your kids off at the front with your mother?" he said since she had locked the car immediately.

"That's right. That way, I can park in the back and leave all the good spots for the moms who need them. That was me for a while."

"I see." He thought it was pretty neat that they'd both had the same idea, but he figured she'd probably just think he was making it up if he said that he'd had that idea too. So he didn't say anything. And they started walking toward the front of the school together.

"I saw that you delivered the roofing and the siding today at some point while I was working."

"This morning. I went and picked it up, but I had to be home because we had a humane inspection at one of our barns and Preston was busy with Gram since she's had her surgery and he's taking care of her."

"I love how you guys just work together. That's neat. A lot of families don't get along."

"We're not any better than most families. We have our differences, but I guess we've just learned that it's more important to be a family than to focus on the things we don't agree about."

"Maybe not having parents helped you with that."

"Probably."

It was so easy to talk to her. Like he didn't have to try to think of things to say.

In fact, he had to sift through the things he wanted to say and think about the most important things. Although, he never felt like he had to keep talking.

Still, normally her kids and her mother were there, and for some reason he didn't want to waste a second of them having complete privacy other than the other shadowy figures who were making their way in from the parking lot. There weren't many this far out, though.

"I know you said your ceiling leaks every time it rains. I was thinking of you some as I was driving here and had determined when I put the roof on the addition, I'll look at it."

"Oh. I hate to ask you to. I did have a tarp on it, but the spring winds blew it off last year, and I just haven't gotten it put back on. I know I need to."

"Yeah. It's important. You end up with mold and weakened and rotting beams."

"Okay. You're scaring me. Making me feel like I should have fixed it months ago. I just didn't—"

"Sorry. Didn't mean to scare you. I'm sure it's fine. But I'll look at it. I guess maybe I was just trying to talk you into letting me."

"I'm talked into it."

They laughed and moved over to the edge of the sidewalk as another couple passed, hurrying back to their car. Probably forgetting something; although, they didn't stop to talk. They just nodded their heads and kept going.

He was clear over on the edge of the sidewalk, but they must not have had enough room because the one who was walking closest to them bumped Shelby's shoulder as she went by.

"I'm so sorry!" the lady called but kept walking.

"It's okay," Shelby said, but she had bumped into him, and his hand landed in the middle of her back, steadying her.

"That's been me more times than I can count," Shelby said, laughing a little as she moved back away from him.

He didn't want to let her go, but after four or five more steps, he dropped his hand.

He wasn't here with her tonight, as much as he might want to be.

"I would imagine it's quite a feat to get three kids ready and take them somewhere without forgetting anything. Especially little ones. It seems like a major ordeal just to get supper on the table."

"It is. It's like that all day long. Of course, I'm working or sleeping a lot while they're up, and I owe my mom more than I could ever repay for watching them for me. I don't know how I could afford it if she didn't."

"Child support?"

He was curious about her husband, but again, this wasn't really the time to ask personal questions.

"He... He had a gambling problem. And he had debts that some pretty powerful people want paid off. You'd think child support would come first, but...it doesn't. Not before gambling debts anyway."

"Wow. That's tough."

"Yeah."

They came around the corner of the building, and he didn't want to leave on such a heavy note, so he said, "Are your kids going to be in costume? Am I going to recognize them? I want to make sure I clap extra loud for them."

"Oh, you know Grace. She'll have every I dotted and every T crossed, and you won't miss her. Haley, on the other hand, if she comes out for her part, it will only be because her teacher prompts her."

They laughed together as he opened the door, and she walked in.

"You're welcome to sit with us if you'd like," she said with a smile on her face and laughter still in her voice.

As she spoke, his eyes landed on Lacey, who stood not at the entrance to the auditorium but at a hallway entrance, like they were going to go in special and not with the rest of the common folk, which he should have known. But she had her hands crossed over her chest and didn't look happy to see him laughing with someone else.

Even though he didn't really consider this a date, she was the one he was there with. Still, there was no harm in laughing with someone else. And he wouldn't feel guilty about it. He hadn't done anything wrong.

"I'm here with Lacey," he said.

Shelby's smile seemed to freeze on her face as her eyes met his, and then she looked around, looking back at him and then following his gaze over to Lacey.

"That's the same girl you were with last Friday night?"

Her question seemed to be laden with undercurrents. An undercurrent that said he was just in her kitchen on Monday evening and told her that he didn't enjoy his date with her, and yet, here he was with her again.

He felt guilty. Mostly because he'd talked badly about Lacey and he shouldn't have.

But also because what he had said was the truth, and instead of living that truth, he'd made excuses and done the easy thing by telling her he'd take her when he shouldn't have. Because it gave people—Shelby—the wrong impression.

"I... I'm here... Yeah. I'm with Lacey. She's the one I was with last Friday. I can explain, but that seems like a line, and it's not."

"I believe you," Shelby said easily, seeming to find her equilibrium again, and as his eyes swept over her face, he didn't see any lingering shock or betrayal or irritation.

Maybe she figured that's just the way everyone was. They talked badly about people behind their backs, then treated them differently to their faces.

That's not the kind of person he wanted to be.

"I'm sorry. I feel like I let you down."

"You didn't. You're just a friend who's doing me a really huge favor, and I would be crazy to be upset with anything you did."

Her words were said easily and didn't seem to have any subtext.

He took them at their surface value.

"I appreciate that. Sometimes it seems like relationships are all drama and no fun."

"I understand. I don't want to be that."

He liked that. Someone who knew what they didn't want to be and took steps to not be it.

"Have fun," Shelby said, giving him a smile and turning toward the doors where everyone else was entering.

He knew he needed to walk toward Lacey. He should be looking at her, but his eyes followed Shelby, her long skirt flowing around her ankles, her heavy coat pulled just a little around her waist, giving the hint of an hourglass figure as she walked away, disappearing into the crowd.

He knew he should be content. Happy with the one he was with. But it was hard to pull his thoughts away from the woman who always made him smile.

Chapter 10

"Mind if I sit here?" The words came in her ear as Shelby finally got her kids seated between her mom on the end and herself in the middle of the row. Their parts weren't until later in the program, and they had to stay in their seats for the first fifteen minutes or so. There was some kind of special award ceremony, which Shelby hoped, for the sake of her children and their inabilities to sit still, didn't drag out too long.

She turned, trying not to disturb Perry who was snuggled down in her lap. The voice was familiar, but she had to crinkle her brows.

Why would Keene be asking to sit beside her? He was here with Lacey.

"Sure. As far as I know, no one is sitting there." The whole rest of the row was empty, and he'd come in from the other side.

"Thanks." He lowered himself to the seat and smiled at her son. "Hey, Perry. You look cozy."

Perry just smiled, comfortable with Keene, not trying to hide his head in her chest like he would have at a stranger.

"Where's Lacey?" she asked. "Isn't that what you said her name was?"

"I did. And yeah. I'm not getting her back for what she did to me. I promise."

"Okay. Good. I wouldn't want to think that you are the vindictive or revengeful type."

"Well, I can't say that I'm perfect in that area, but I do try to treat people the way I want to be treated, not the way I feel like treating them."

"Nice," she said, thinking about the whole reason they were here—the birth of Christ and the love that the Father had and what it all represented. If there were any place she could try to think about doing good, it should be here.

"She's going to take part in the ceremony at the beginning. And they actually have seats blocked off in front for those people." He grunted. "They have one for me too, but I feel a little pretentious sitting in the very important people seats, so I thought I'd come back here and sit where I felt like I belonged."

"I think you belong a little further up than here with me," she said, smiling and meaning it.

"I can't imagine I would have more fun with anyone else, so maybe it's less about where I feel like I belong and more about where I want to be."

She closed her mouth. She didn't really have anything to say to that.

He'd just said he wanted to sit with her. That was crazy.

"It's kinda funny that you're escorting Lacey and want to sit with my children. I can let you borrow them if you'd like." That had to be what he meant. He wanted to hang out with her kids. There was definitely a lot of kid in him. She'd figured that out from the three evening meals they'd eaten together.

"I do like your kids. A lot. They're fun, but I like their mom, too."

Perry wiggled on her lap, and Shelby was grateful for the distraction. She didn't know what to say to that. He'd kind of rendered her speechless.

"I guess I don't understand. It's odd that you'd want to sit back here but you're with someone else."

"I know. I feel guilty because I couldn't explain it all to you, and I guess I should have spent the time that we were walking in talking about it instead of whatever we talked about."

He explained a little about how Lacey had texted him and how he hadn't wanted to tell her flat-out no because of all the things she'd said.

"As soon as we walked in and I saw her, I knew I would rather just go on and be with you. I should have been honest to begin with and just told her no. But the fact that she told other people she couldn't go with them because she was expecting to go with me made me feel like

I kind of had to take her or she'd end up by herself and it would be my fault."

"I see."

She didn't know what else to say. She liked that he didn't want to hurt her feelings, but she felt like it was always more important to be honest. Even if someone's feelings were hurt, at least they weren't deceived.

Which was worse?

To her, hurting someone's feelings wasn't necessarily a sin, but deceitfulness most definitely was.

"If I had to do it over again, I would have called her and been honest on the phone. But it's a lesson learned. Kinda funny because after the date we had last week, I would have thought she'd never talk to me again, so the whole thing took me by surprise."

"I think women can be weird that way."

"I think women can be weird in a lot of different ways, no offense."

"None taken. Because you're right." They grinned at each other, and Shelby didn't have any thought in her head of defending her gender. It was true. Sometimes women could just be weird or downright dumb. "But the same thing is true of men."

"At least we're straight-line. Women are... I don't even know. I don't even know of anything that's curly enough to be compared to a woman."

"A strand of cooked spaghetti?" Shelby offered helpfully.

"I'm not even sure that works."

"I guess I have to agree. Unless it's tied in a knot."

"In several different places."

"You almost have me convinced you don't like women."

"That might be partially true. I definitely am not a love-all-the-women-in-the-world kind of man. I think I'm more of a one-woman guy."

She wasn't quite sure what that meant. Maybe he'd had his heart broken and had given up on women. She hadn't heard, but she'd been gone from Prairie Rose for a lot of years.

They didn't have a chance to say anything more because it was then that her girls stopped rubbernecking and looking for all their friends and saw that Mr. Keene was sitting beside their mom. Both of them hopped out of their seats and went over, standing in front of him, chattering about what they were going to be doing, and telling him how excited they were that he came, and eventually both of them ended up in his lap, one on each knee.

Shelby knew she shouldn't do it, but she glanced over at her mom, who had her eyebrows raised and an I-told-you-so look on her face.

Shelby really wanted to lean across the seat and say "he's here with another woman," just to see the look disappear from her mom's face, but that wouldn't be nice, not to her mom, and not to Keene either, who had taken the time to explain what was really going on.

She wasn't quite sure why he had done that, but she supposed it really didn't matter.

She didn't have to analyze everything. She could just live and be happy. And take things as they came. Take the friendship that Keene had offered and return it. Not looking to see if there was anything more, hoping that there was, or worrying about whether she was reading everything right.

It was a whole new train of thought for her, but she felt it was a good one. And right.

After the principal had gotten his award, Shelby's daughters left, making their way up to the back of the stage while everyone clapped, and Lacey stood onstage beaming, looking like a natural in her role.

"She's beautiful," Shelby couldn't help but say as Keene leaned into her.

He stopped, blinked, and then looked up at the stage.

He looked back at her and said, "I guess she is." He paused as though maybe her comment had scattered his thoughts, and then he said, "Thanks for letting me sit here. I wish I could stay."

"It's good to talk to you," she said, feeling a little bit awkward. What did one say to a man who was leaving one and going to someone else?

Maybe she wanted to repeat or echo his words, telling him she wished he could stay. Which was true, but it just didn't seem right.

She met his eyes, their faces close as the applause died down and he really had to go.

"Maybe we'll meet in the parking lot later."

She was about to say she had three children and she wasn't meeting anyone anywhere, but then she realized they were parked side by side, and so she said, "Maybe."

She kind of hoped so but also kind of didn't. He was leaving with someone else. And she didn't want to think about that.

So she focused on the program and didn't even watch as he walked away.

The program went a lot longer than what she was expecting, longer than it had in years past. Maybe it was the awards that had been given out at the beginning, but regardless, she was checking the time quite frequently till it was finally over.

She needed to be at work in twenty minutes, and it took ten for her to walk from the parking lot to the convenience store.

She didn't want to leave without helping her mom get the kids in the car since Perry had fallen asleep on her chest and would need to be carried out.

"I'm not feeling very well," her mom whispered to her as the kids onstage were singing the last song, "We Wish You a Merry Christmas."

"Like you're sick in the stomach?" she asked, wondering if they might have gotten something from Keene. Although, that was last week that he had been sick.

"No, I'm just feeling sore all over and weak. I think it might be my fibromyalgia kicking in."

"I can't let you take the kids home by yourself." Sometimes her mom would be in bed for days. She could usually handle the children as long as she didn't have to take them anywhere, but getting them into the car would be tough, and Shelby didn't want to risk having her drive. When she was having a flare-up, she never did.

"If you try to go home, you're going to be late for work."

She hated to get up and walk out before it was quite over, but if she hurried, she might be able to at least get the kids inside the car, and maybe her mom could handle it from there.

She whispered to her mom that she was going to go out and get the car and she'd be around the building.

"Don't try to lift Perry. I'll be back in to get him."

Her mom looked at her with grateful eyes and just nodded.

Typically during a flare-up, she was exhausted.

Feeling bad for the people behind her, Shelby got up and stepped around her mom, hurrying down the aisle to get out of people's way, hoping she didn't get in anybody's video.

It felt like forever until she opened the outside door and stepped out onto the sidewalk. She began to jog.

"Hey!" Steps on the sidewalk sounded behind her.

She recognized his voice but stopped and turned around anyway. "Keene. You're trying to get a jump on the crowd?"

"No. I saw you leaving and wondered if there was something wrong. Maybe you're trying to get a jump on the crowd?"

"Kind of. Mom isn't feeling well, and I think it's her fibromyalgia flaring up. I was going to have her take the kids home and put them to bed while I walked to work, but I hate to leave her with all of that when she's not feeling well. I'm going to be late to work, and I hate that, but I need to get my kids home safely. And I need to take care of Mom, too."

Chapter 11

Shelby hated that she always felt like she was struggling between trying to get her bills paid and being a responsible adult, taking care of her family. It felt like there was never a middle ground that she could walk easily. She was always pulled toward one side or the other.

She'd already been late for work twice in the last three months. She didn't think she'd get fired if she was late again, but she supposed it was possible they would strip her manager position from her, which would mean less money.

"Let me help." Keene spoke softly but insistently.

"You can't help. You have a date." Surely he remembered that as they power walked toward the vehicles. She thought it would be rude for her to jog beside him, so she was just walking as fast as she could.

"She'll understand. She'll help."

Shelby highly doubted that, but if Keene would help her with her kids, she wouldn't be late.

She was tempted to take him up on it.

"No. I can't. It's tempting. I'd really like to, but I can't allow you to do that. You're already spending all of your free time at my house building an addition. I can't let you do more for me."

"You're not letting me. I'm insisting. Give me the keys to your car."

"I have time to help get the kids in the car."

"Go back inside and help them out. Help your mom. I'll bring the car around."

"What about Lacey?"

"I'll text her."

She kept her mouth shut over that. Shelby didn't have his number. So he couldn't text her. Which was fine, since she wasn't on a date with him. Just...he'd have her kids.

He'd be with her mom, though. She could text her mom if she needed anything.

Although, holding the phone and moving her thumbs over the small screen was sometimes difficult for her mom.

She could call her.

Man, she was a mess. Anxious over her mom and her kids and her job and unable to get her mind off of Keene who somehow kept showing up beside her.

Like her thinking about him conjured him up.

"Shelby?" he said, still walking beside her, adjusting his steps to hers.

"I'm sorry. You're right." She stopped, digging in her purse. "I'll go get the kids, and we'll be waiting on the far side of the school so you can just pull alongside, and I'll help you get the kids in before I get Mom. And I can help Lacey find us?"

"Perfect. Don't worry. I'll take care of Lacey."

She smiled a little, not wanting to be the reason that he ditched his date. Although, there was a part of her that said the last time he was out with Lacey, she ditched him.

That didn't make it right, and she didn't want that for this time.

She pulled her keys out of her purse and handed them over. His fingers didn't just brush hers, they cradled hers for a moment, and she almost thought it was on purpose.

Her eyes flew to his even as she had started to turn away. She froze. Her breath caught. And then her heart, already pounding in her chest from the fast walking that she had been doing, started doing something even faster.

He was too nice. He was being too nice to her. She wasn't going to be able to keep from wanting more. Wanting to be more than just friends.

"Thanks," she said, ripping her eyes away, and pulling her hand back, and hurrying down the sidewalk from which they'd just come. She wanted to get in before they let out and she had to fight against the crowd to get to her kids.

If he said anything in response, she didn't hear it.

Thankfully, as she walked in, someone else was being awarded the Poinsettias that were sitting at the front of the auditorium. Then there were a few announcements that droned on as she softly walked to her mom and then whispered in her ear, "I'll take the girls and Perry out, and I'll come back for you. Just hold tight."

It spoke to how terrible her mom felt when she just nodded.

She motioned to the girls, who sleepily got up to follow her.

Normally, by this time they were all tucked in bed and she was heading to work.

She reached the door, Perry in her arms; she turned and went backward, pushing with the small of her back against the handle.

She almost fell as it was pulled away from her.

"Here. I've got him. Where's your mom?"

"Still in her seat. Girls, follow Mr. Keene."

Grace nodded, but Haley looked at her, rubbing one eye. Her brows furrowed.

"Come here, Haley. I'll carry you," Keene said, already having shifted Perry to one arm. He reached down and scooped Haley up.

Shelby caught just a glimpse of her smile as her daughter lifted her head and snuggled into Keene's chest.

She couldn't bear to look him in the eyes, so she turned without saying anything or looking at him again and hurried back in, knowing that bringing her mom out would be a much slower process.

Her mom had stood up and had only made it to the edge of her seat.

"Lean on me, Mom," she whispered as other people were starting to drift out.

Her mom's steps were slow, shuffling, painful, but Shelby had her arm around her, and they made it to the door before the audience clapped at what Shelby assumed was the very end.

Again, Keene was waiting and pulled the door away from her back.

"I have the kids in the car; if you want to walk over and say goodbye to them, I'll help your mom."

He slipped around the other side of her mom, and Shelby, rather than leaving, figured it would be easier for her mom to have support on both sides.

Keene's arm crossed over hers, and he seemed to pick up a little, holding some of the weight from her mom's feet and helping her mom to go a little faster. As they reached her car, Shelby slipped away and opened the front door.

"Can you make it in, Mom?"

"I feel terrible that I'm causing you all of this trouble."

"No trouble."

"No trouble at all. You're making an old fella feel useful."

Shelby grinned at that, and even her mom smiled. Like Keene was going around trying to find things to make him feel useful.

Keene helped her mom in while Shelby opened the back door, leaning way over and kissing Perry's sleeping head before giving Grace and Haley hugs and telling them to be good.

She hated leaving them, but she needed to get to work.

"I wish there was enough room. I would drive you to work."

"I'll be fine."

"How are you getting home?"

"Normally Mom comes and picks me up, but I can get someone else to take me home."

"I'll do it. What time?"

"You don't have to. I can get someone. You've already done enough."

"What time?"

"Don't you have farm work to do in the morning?"

"It's not like milking cows. I can do the eggs anytime. Tell me what time I can pick you up."

"Keene?" a voice behind them said. Keene's eyes didn't move from hers, and she didn't turn around to look, either.

"Tell me."

"Eight o'clock," she said and watched as an expression of satisfaction crossed his face before he nodded.

"I'll be there at seven forty-five." He paused. "And...and I'd really like it if you'd text me and let me know you get there okay."

"Keene? I thought you said that you would be right back. You haven't even left yet!" Lacey's voice cut through their conversation, irritated and put out.

"I just got Miss Cindy into the car. I'm going to take her home, then I'll be back for you." He looked over at Shelby. "I forgot to ask permission to drive your car around. Just back to the school, and I'll use my truck to take Lacey home."

It would only be twenty minutes to go home and come back, but Shelby still felt bad that Lacey would have to wait. Although if it were her, she didn't really think she would mind if her date was helping a sick woman and her grandchildren home.

"Your number?" Keene asked, his brows lifted, his hand slowly pulling his phone out of his pocket, wanting to make sure that she was okay with giving him her number. She appreciated that he wasn't pushing for that like he'd pushed her for a time to pick her up.

She nodded, wanting to make sure her children got home, and part of her wanted his number. A big part of her.

She rattled her number off, and he typed it in as fast as she said it.

"I sent you a text."

Her phone buzzed as he said it, and she said, "Thanks." She turned toward Lacey and lifted a hand. "Thank you so much for donating a little bit of your evening so that he can take my mom and kids home. I really appreciate it."

"What is he to you?" Lacey asked, ignoring her words.

"I'm his charity case," Shelby said, not meaning it in a derogatory way but knowing what she said was true. He'd been donating a lot of his time for her because she hadn't been able to stand on her own two feet.

Someday.

When she said that, Lacey's eyes grew shrewd as she looked at the uniform that Shelby wore. A smug look settled across her face. "I see."

Shelby imagined that if Lacey were looking into a hogpen, she'd probably use the same tone to talk to the mother sow.

"That's not true," Keene said, and it sounded like his teeth were clenched.

"I need to run," she said, looking at Lacey and then starting off. She was tempted to issue another thank you, but she wasn't super happy with the way the evening had gone—worried about her mom, concerned about her children, and feeling terrible that she'd once again come between Keene and his date.

Even if she believed he was being honest when he said that he hadn't really wanted to go with her, it still didn't sit right, coming between them.

As she hurried along the front of the building, dodging folks who were walking out, she pulled her phone out of her purse and looked at the screen. She smiled at what he had written.

Don't forget to text me when you get there.

It'd been a long time since anyone cared that much about her, and she had to admit it felt good.

Chapter 12

At seven forty the next morning, Keene pulled into the convenience store where Shelby worked. He'd been pretty pushy the night before, and he felt bad. Not bad that he'd gotten what he wanted but that he hadn't had time to be a little more caring and a little less insistent.

She'd texted like he'd asked her to when she made it to the store, and he'd texted her when he'd gotten home and had the children in bed before he left to go back and get Lacey. To his surprise, Lacey had waited, standing with a group of friends, chatting and laughing.

In fact, after he got there, it was another twenty-five minutes before she was ready to leave.

Part of him suspected she made him wait because he'd made her wait first.

It didn't matter if she was a tit-for-tat kind of person, that was fine. He had no intentions of ever going out with her again.

He filled up his pickup with fuel at the pump, paying there before walking into the convenience store.

Shelby looked dead on her feet to him, and he tried to shove aside the instinct to ask her to slow down. It really was none of his business. Although, maybe if he kept coming around, they'd become good enough friends that maybe she'd allow him to make a few suggestions about how she should be taking care of herself.

"Good morning," she said with a smile that was way too chipper for someone who had stayed up all night.

"Good morning. Although it's overcast and we're expecting a snowstorm, it's still a pretty good morning," he said, nodding at the younger woman who was running the cash register beside Shelby's.

"I have a couple of things I need to do, and then I'll be out," she said, doing something with her cash register and then waiting for his nod before she spoke to the girl working with her.

It wasn't long until she was back out, the apron she'd been wearing taken off, and her hat gone as well, carrying a bag with what looked like milk and maybe bananas.

Her smile still looked fresh, though, even if her eyes seemed droopy and her face drawn.

"Are you driving my car?" she asked.

He pushed the door open and held it for her while she walked through.

After he walked through, he answered, "No. I thought I'd drop you off at the school so you could drive it home. If that's okay."

"Of course. Whatever works for you. I was wondering how I would get it back."

"I'll follow you home, though. You have to be tired after being up all night."

"Oh, this isn't as bad as it usually is. Because of the storm coming, the country club is closed. Normally I would go there after here and work on the breakfast cleanup and some lunch prep before I'd go home and catch a nap."

"Don't you think you might be working a little bit much?" Keene snapped his mouth shut as soon as the words were out. He knew he shouldn't have said anything.

"I have to." She didn't sound upset, maybe just sad.

He glanced over at her, but her eyes were scanning the parking lot until she saw his truck, and then they dropped to the ground as they walked toward it.

He didn't say anything more until they reached the truck, going to the passenger side and opening her door so she could get in.

"Thank you," she murmured as she adjusted her purse and stepped up.

He waited until she was settled and reaching for her seatbelt before he slammed her door shut.

She hadn't agreed, but she hadn't gotten mad, either.

Once he got in and got settled with his belt on, he started carefully backing out of the parking lot. "Lacey knows I'm not going out with her again. I just... I just wanted to let you know."

She nodded but didn't say anything, and he let it go.

Maybe she wasn't interested. She obviously was busy, but he felt bad for the way he had seemed to be juggling two women yesterday. It hadn't been something he'd ever done before, and he definitely didn't want to do it again. He had learned his lesson, and if he didn't want to go out with someone, he wasn't going to say yes, no matter how they phrased it.

Especially when there was someone else he had his eye on.

He'd be lying to say that he didn't want to have his eye on Shelby. Seeing her having to leave and go to work had been hard. She'd been tired, and she'd been walking the way she did when her back hurt.

"You said the country club was canceled and you wouldn't be working there today. But the snow is supposed to start this evening. What about the convenience store? Are you still scheduled?"

"Yes, in fact, the convenience store will probably be extra busy tonight because of people walking in and picking up milk and eggs in preparation for the storm." She laughed a little and then said, "Oh! I forgot." She held up the bag that she'd been carrying. "Can we stop at Miss Ginny's house? You don't have to. I can double back after we get my car."

"Of course, I can stop. She doesn't have any family in town. It wouldn't hurt to check on her before the storm hits."

"Of course." She laughed a little. "I kind of forgot she went to your church."

"She's a good lady."

"She is. Reggie usually gets her groceries, but on Saturdays I make sure she has some fresh milk and a couple of bananas to get her through the rest of the week."

"That's awfully nice of you."

She seemed to shrug off his praise and didn't say anything. Although, her fingers fiddled with the handle of the bag.

There was silence while he negotiated the streets of Prairie Rose, heading toward Miss Ginny's house.

He had wanted to talk to Shelby, so he forced himself to open his mouth and say, "It's supposed to be snowing tonight. I'd really like it if you'd let me take you to the convenience store whenever you have to be there."

"I start work at eleven, and no. I can't let you come out here in the middle of the night just to take me to work. It's not that far, and I can do it."

"I figured that's what you'd say, but it would really make me feel a lot better if you'd change your mind."

"I can text you when I get there again safely if that will ease your mind some. But it would make me feel terrible if you're out in the middle of the night because of me."

"You're out."

"I have to work."

"And I don't. So I have time to take you."

"We can argue about this if you want to."

"I think we already are."

"We don't seem upset. Don't people who are having arguments have to be upset with each other?"

"I think we can have a civil argument, can't we?"

"Is that what this is? Civil?" She laughed as though the idea of a civil argument wasn't one that she'd ever considered before.

"It is. Because neither one of us is going to get upset about it." And he liked that. He liked that they could have a discussion where they completely disagreed but that they respected each other's opinions and respected each other as adults and neither one of them insisted that they had to have their way. "But I can try to change your mind."

"And I can refuse to have my mind changed." There was humor in her voice but also maybe a question. Like she wasn't used to a man who wasn't going to get upset with her if she didn't agree with every word that came out of his mouth.

He supposed he could see where that attitude came from. He knew a lot of men, and some women, too, who couldn't stand to have anyone disagree with them. Who couldn't be friends with someone they didn't agree with. Seemed to him that kinda defeated the purpose of friendship. Or, at least, it wasn't a true friendship. If he couldn't love someone no matter what they believed, no matter what they did, no matter what they said, then it wasn't a true friendship. Not a true love. Not to him.

"If you go silent, does that mean I win?"

"So now we have winners and losers?"

"Doesn't an argument have to have a winner?"

"Can't we call it a draw?"

"So I suppose you're one of those people that think everyone should get a participation trophy?"

He laughed. "You have me there. I'm most definitely not one of those people. Competition is good. Baseball games wouldn't be nearly as interesting if they didn't keep score."

She laughed too, but then she sobered as they pulled off the street in front of Miss Ginny's house. "I guess that's life, too. Right? We don't get participation trophies. Those of us who make bad decisions just pay for it over and over again."

"I don't think life is a competition. At least I don't see it that way. I think a lot of bad decisions can be overcome, and it's not really about the things that seem to be important."

"Seem to be?" she said, sounding skeptical. "You mean are."

"No. Not really. I mean, you have to eat, you have to take care of your children, but that takes less than what we think, and the things that really matter—pleasing God and loving other people—are the true markers of success."

He could tell by the expression on her face that she didn't agree with him, but he'd pulled the pickup to a stop, and she shrugged her shoulders, her hand on the door latch.

"You don't have to come in. I can be fast."

"If you don't mind, I'll run in and say hi and see if she needs me to do anything to get her ready for the storm. Don't worry, if she has anything for me to do that will take a long time, I'll take you home first. You have to be tired and ready for bed."

"Usually it takes a little bit to get wound down after coming home from work. But yeah, I'm tired."

She pulled her door latch, and they got out together.

Chapter 13

It was easy for someone who wasn't struggling to pay his bills to say that the most important thing in life was pleasing God and loving others.

But she couldn't expect someone like Keene—who hadn't made the bad decisions that she had—to understand.

She was intrigued by his thoughts, though, and wanted to ponder the idea some. But her thoughts were interrupted because he didn't go to the front door like she usually did. They walked along the side of the house on a narrow walkway that led to the back door.

She'd been bringing Miss Ginny milk and bananas for a while, and they'd chatted a few times, but Shelby never had a whole lot of time to sit and talk.

Keene stopped at the back door, rapped sharply a few times, then twisted the knob and pushed it open, calling out, "Hello, the house," as he walked in.

He held the door while she followed, and she appreciated the fact that he hadn't made her walk first into this lady's house when she hadn't answered the door. That would have been a little uncomfortable.

Miss Ginny was just standing up from the kitchen table where her Bible lay spread out in front of her, a notebook to the side with notes in an elegant hand taking up half the page.

"Keene! I wasn't expecting you this morning." Then her eyes fell on Shelby. "And you brought the hardest-working lady in town with you." Her smile grew even more if that were possible, and she held her arms out to Shelby. "I'm so happy to see you, my dear."

She walked carefully forward, and Shelby hurried to her, trying to keep her from having to move more than necessary. Shelby hugged the older lady, enjoying the slight scent of yeast and cinnamon and comfort and safety and peace.

"Miss Ginny," Keene said as Shelby pulled back and the older woman straightened. "How come you're greeting her with more enthusiasm than you greet me? You had me in Sunday School when I was still in diapers."

"Come here, boy, let me give you a hug too," she said, a little tease in her voice as she sounded put out, but Shelby knew she was anything but.

Keene walked over and bent down and hugged Miss Ginny while Shelby took the milk out of the bag and put it in the refrigerator and set the bananas on the counter.

"Is there anything you need me to do? Anything in particular because of the snow coming, or anything quick while I'm here?"

"Well, I was just sitting here thinking about the snow shovels in the shed outside. They're probably behind the lawnmower and the hedge trimmers by now and who knows what else. But I'm thinking I'll need them, and as much snow as we were supposed to get, I thought it might be kind of hard to open the shed doors if I didn't get them out before it started."

"I'll go out and do that for you. It shouldn't take too long even if I have to move the lawnmower. Is that okay with you, Shelby?"

He said her name, and something odd but not unpleasant struck down her backbone. "Of course. Please." She turned toward Miss Ginny. "Is there anything I can do to help?"

"You just sit down and keep me company while Keene goes out and does that. That'll be the best help you can do."

Shelby smiled and pulled out the chair that Miss Ginny indicated while Keene walked to the door and disappeared through it. Miss Ginny settled herself in her chair, and they started off chatting about the weather and the storm that was coming.

"I just love sitting and watching the snow come down from my front window," Miss Ginny said, sounding almost dreamy.

"I love watching it snow too. The kids get so excited and always want to go out and play even before there's anything on the ground to play in. And then I always try to have hot chocolate too. It just makes it fun."

"That's right. Kids make everything fun. Especially snow." Miss Ginny smiled, and then her look grew serious. "How are you holding up? You have a lot on your plate and a lot of burdens to bear."

Normally Shelby would smile and say she was fine. But maybe it was because she hadn't had much sleep because of the school play last night, or maybe it was just because of being around Keene and wanting more than what she had, not really being satisfied with what she'd been given.

Maybe she was just tired.

That must have been it, since Miss Ginny's words caused tears to prick at the back of her eyes.

"Oh, honey," Miss Ginny said, leaning over and putting an arm around Shelby's shoulders.

Shelby leaned on the soft shoulder and fought the tightness in her throat. "Sometimes I wonder... Like, I know that a lot of the problems I have are because of choices I made. But a lot of the bills I'm paying, a lot of the reason I have to have two jobs, is because my husband was addicted to gambling and he used credit cards that were just in my name to pay his bills. I'm stuck with paying them off, and it seems so unfair."

"That doesn't seem fair to me either," Miss Ginny said as she stroked Shelby's shoulder. She let those words hang in the kitchen for a bit, and then she said, "But I suppose you know that God allows trials for us even when they're not fair because He knows that's what we need."

"Sometimes I think God hates me."

"Oh, child, He doesn't. I promise He doesn't. He loves you more than you can believe. Just... Just sometimes you know you look at your kids and you understand that they have to go through these hard things, like first days of kindergarten, or bullies on the playground, or work they don't understand. Potty training. Watching their mom leave.

All things that are hard for kids but that help them to grow into adults that are able to handle things."

"I know. I just feel like bad thing after bad thing happens. Why?"

"You know, anything that happens to you could be the best thing that ever happens to you." Miss Ginny squeezed her hand while her words tripped around in Shelby's head. That sounded so optimistic. She wanted to believe it.

"And the best way to deal with the bad things is to accept them. They are what they are. And just be at peace. Knowing that God has them in your life for a reason. It doesn't help with the tiredness, but it should help with the guilt. Should help with the questions as to why, or the feelings of unfairness, and also the idea that your bad decisions are all at fault. God could have changed those if He wanted. But He allowed them, and without those bad decisions, you wouldn't be where you are. Possibly on the cusp of something really beautiful, but you can't see it."

"Well, that's true at least. I definitely can't see it."

"Maybe God has a little bit of growing for you to do. Maybe He's got something beautiful right around the corner, and all He wants for you to do is draw a little closer to Him."

It wasn't exactly what Keene had just gotten done saying before they got out of the pickup. About the most important things in life being drawing closer to God and loving other people, but maybe God was nudging her. Maybe He really did want her to grow a little before He could bless her.

"So I thought of trials and how they test us, but I guess sometimes God gives us trials to grow us, too?"

"That's exactly right. He wants us to live in gratitude and appreciation. Maybe that's something He wants us to learn through our trials. I know as I get older, and I'm able to do less and less, as I'm not a young girl anymore, and I can't work all day, I don't have a husband to share things with anymore, and just getting up from a chair is a trial. It's been harder and harder to have appreciation and gratitude. Old age itself is a trial. But I know God wants me to smile. He wants me to be happy, joyful. He wants me to grow closer to Him and love the people around me. When I was younger, loving the people around me maybe meant doing things for them or spending time with them, but now maybe it means praying for them. I've got plenty of time to pray. All I have to do is turn my TV off and walk away from the Internet."

"Sometimes that's hard."

"It sure is. Actually, most of the time I'd rather read a book than pray. But I believe in the power of prayer. But not thinking about yourself, and thinking about others instead, doesn't get any easier as you get older. It's a muscle that you have to flex."

"That's funny. Keene said something very similar to that to me not fifteen minutes ago, and I kind of shrugged it off."

"Well, maybe he's a little wiser than we give him credit for. By thinking about others, accepting what is, whether it's getting older, or whether it's bills that you have to pay, and being at peace with what's in your life, trusting that God hasn't forgotten about you and that He's working out the best for you—gonna work it out for your good—are lessons we can learn at any age. Mine or yours."

"Those things sound so easy. I mean, what could be easier than just accepting what is and being at peace? But to actually do that?"

"It requires a lot more faith than what most people have. Because you need to trust God. But sometimes God's ideas aren't ideas that we think are any good."

"So true. I just know they're going to be more work or more suffering or require more of me, more of me than I want to give because I want to keep it for myself."

"Exactly. It's funny, though, the doctor will say, well, you need to take chemo, and even though it's hard, we go through it because the doctor says to." Miss Ginny shook her head. "Why don't we trust God that much?"

"That's a good question. A good point." Shelby thought of all the things the doctors had told her mom she needed to do for fibromyalgia. Food she needed to eat, and lifestyle changes she had to make. And for the most part, her mom did them all. As much as she could. Yet, to relax and be at peace with the circumstances in her life and just trust God to work things out for her good, was almost more than she could do.

"You know, I can see just from our conversation that my faith isn't nearly what it needs to be." She straightened a little. "But the thing that really struck me is what you said about how anything that happens to you could be the best thing that ever happens to you. That's not just positive thinking. That's faith. Faith that God can work everything out for your good. Through anything that happens."

"That's exactly right. So your ex-husband was a gambler. Maybe that'll be the best thing that ever happened to you."

"Sometimes I just wish God worked a little faster. It would be easier to have faith if His timeline was a little shorter."

"We're not looking for easy. It's the hard stuff that grows you."

"Hey, ladies," Keene said as he walked back in the door. "I put the shovels on the front porch, both of them, and moved the snowblower so it's beside the front door. Maybe you forgot you had it?"

"I did, actually. Preston bought that for me on clearance last spring, and I'd completely forgotten about it. I don't suppose I can do the steps with it, but it'll help with the sidewalks."

"Sure will. Kind of looks fun. I might have to swing around here tomorrow when the snow starts coming down just so I can take it for a test drive."

"Just like a man. Give them something with a motor, and they can't wait to go play." Miss Ginny smiled at Keene, who grinned, looking just as guilty as he probably was.

"Are you ready?" he asked, looking at Shelby.

She leaned over, putting her arm around Miss Ginny again and leaning into her. "Thank you."

Some words of wisdom from a lady who had been through a lot worse than she had was exactly what she'd needed to shift her outlook and help her to realize that the next best thing could be right around the corner; all she had to do was just trust that God was working everything for her good and His glory.

Chapter 14

It was eight o'clock in the morning when Shelby pulled into her unplowed spot next to the trailer.

The snow was still coming down even though almost two feet lay on the ground.

The convenience store had actually shut down when her shift left because another foot was forecast to fall and nobody except essential workers were to be traveling.

She managed to get her car off the road but not parked up where she normally did. She turned it off anyway.

It was going to be really difficult to shovel this. Heavy and wet, the snow was typical of what often fell when the temperatures hovered right around freezing.

Just a few degrees warmer, and they'd be dealing with a lot of rain.

She grabbed her purse and pulled her phone out of the cupholder. It had buzzed with a text on her way home, and part of her hoped it might be Keene. He'd texted last night asking her to let him know she'd gotten safely to work, which she had.

It wouldn't surprise her at all if he texted asking her to let him know she'd gotten safely home.

There was a certain amount of comfort in his texts. If she had gotten stuck along the road, if she had any trouble at all, she knew he'd find a way to her and help.

How long had it been since someone had her back like that?

She had friends in college who would be really irritated with those texts, but to her, it meant someone cared about her. She'd been alone long enough that she appreciated it.

Okay, maybe she liked the man behind them, too.

Deciding she'd sit in her car and answer since she saw the light in the kitchen window and her mom standing at the sink and knew that once she stepped in, she'd be drawn into the life of her family and wouldn't have time to text, she opened her phone and clicked on his message.

Later, she wasn't sure what caught her eye, but she remembered looking out the windshield, her eyes fixed on the trailer as she thought about what to say.

Like it was happening in slow motion, she saw the roof, burdened by the weight of the two feet of snow that sat on it, slowly cave in until it disappeared from sight. A muffled thump and crash came through her car, and the back of her trailer, from about the spot where the roof leaked to the end which encompassed almost all of her mom's bedroom, no longer had a roof with two feet of snow on it.

It had nothing, except walls.

Her eyes widened, and her brain raced even as she threw her phone back in her purse and grabbed the latch on her door.

Her mom was in the kitchen. She had just seen her head. The kids were sleeping at the other end of the trailer. No one should have gotten hurt. That was her first and main concern. But other questions swirled, too.

What was she going to do? Where was she going to live? This was the cheapest place she could find, and she could barely afford it. How were they going to stay warm with no roof? Could they stay in the trailer? What about Christmas? She was already living with her mother. She'd run out of options. There were no more.

As she was hopping through the deep snow, carefully, trying not to fall and also trying not to get any more of it on herself than necessary since she was no longer going to have a warm house to thaw out in, she stopped short, her hand on the banister and one foot on the rickety steps. On the steps that used to be rickety, but at some point, Keene had fixed them, bracing them somehow and making it so the entire set-up didn't shake as one walked up and down on it.

She hadn't even gotten to thank him for it. But that wasn't what stopped her. It was the thought. The one that she'd been thinking about and talking to Miss Ginny about yesterday. It went through her brain so crystal clear it was almost like someone had spoken it right next to her ear.

Anything that happens to you could be the best thing that ever happens to you.

She almost laughed. This close, she couldn't really see the total lack of a roof. Just the snow sticking up above the walls right in front of her and moving on for another five feet before it stopped abruptly.

The roof of her trailer caving in could be the best thing that ever happened?

But suddenly, instead of fear. Instead of panic. Instead of the total freak-out that had been happening in her chest, a peace settled down. She could almost feel it move from the top of her body to the bottom, cooling her veins, easing her heartbeat, settling her lungs. A peace that, no matter what happened, God was in control. All she had to do was accept what had happened and be at peace with it.

The loss of her home. The uncertainty of where she would live. Even the suffering, and Heaven forbid, the possible death of one of her children.

No matter what happened, God had it. The thought that time could be of the essence hadn't left her brain, but her hand was not shaking as she gripped the doorknob and turned, opening the door and stepping into the kitchen where her mother stood at the doorway of the small dining area, looking down the hall, her hand at her throat, her eyes wide as they lifted, jerking back and taking in Shelby.

"Did you see that?" her mother asked breathlessly.

"I did. I heard a little too." Her voice, calm, almost felt surreal. Why was she not more upset? "Are the children still in bed?"

Her mother nodded, a little bit of confusion clouding the shocked look on her face.

"Mommy?" Grace stood at the other end of the living room, at the entrance to the hall, rubbing her eyes, her face pinched and unsure. "I thought someone was shooting at me."

Shelby stamped her feet on the rug, getting most of the snow off, then walked across the kitchen and living room, bending down in front of her daughter and wrapping her arms around her. Thankful that the Lord hadn't seen fit to make the trial about taking her children.

Although, with this new peace that settled inside of her, she knew, if He had, it would have been okay.

"No one's shooting, sweetheart. There was just a lot of snow on the roof, and it caved in."

Then a thought struck her. If that part of the roof had caved in, maybe she should be shoveling the snow off of the rest of the roof.

Of course, there was the leak. That had probably weakened some of the support. Still. If they were going to be living here, she'd better get the rest of the snow off.

"What are we going to do?" her mother asked, coming forward, slowly, as though her joints still ached.

"I'm going to pray about it," she said, although, she wasn't sure where the words came from. She'd never really responded like that before. But that seemed like the thing to do.

So, before anyone could say anything else, she bowed her head and whispered just a few words, asking the Lord to give her wisdom and thanking Him for the absolute peace that she felt the whole way to her innermost soul.

This was going to be okay. Of course it was going to be okay. God had orchestrated it, and He wasn't in the business of doing things for the kicks and giggles. He was going to do it for her. Her benefit. For her growth and His glory.

She said amen and looked up. Waiting for the answer to just fall on her head like the peace had.

After about ten seconds, Grace said, "Mommy? I'm cold."

Of course, she was. There was a big hole in their house, and heat was escaping even though the furnace was running.

"Let me set you on the couch with Grammy. I'll grab a blanket for you both, and you can snuggle. Maybe she'll even let you watch cartoons."

Talk about fiddling while Rome burned.

Wasn't there something weird about having the TV on while snow blew in through the big hole in the ceiling?

At least the small Christmas tree over on the edge of the living room against the wall might actually have a few real snow flurries on it. That could only improve the decorating job that she and her children had done.

"I think I have a tarp in the shed. I'll go look and see if I can pin it up to at least cover the hole."

As she walked through the kitchen, digging in her pockets for gloves which she hadn't bothered to put on when she left work, she heard her phone buzzing from where it sat in her purse on the counter. She hadn't even realized she'd set her purse down there.

It reminded her that Keene had texted her and she'd been in the process of responding when the roof had fallen in.

What was she going to say to him? "Do you know of a place where we can live that's really, really cheap but also big enough for a woman and her mother and her three children?"

Still, she dug in her purse for her phone, shoving it in her back pocket before she walked out.

She had to kick the snow away from the doors of the shed before she was able to open them, and even then, the ground had frozen in lumpy bumps that made trying to get the doors open an exercise in perseverance.

It must have taken twenty minutes to get the doors open, and when she did, she remembered that she had moved the Christmas gifts the church had donated for the children out here when they'd realized that they would never be able to hide them from the children in her mother's bedroom.

At least they weren't ruined by the snow falling in.

She smiled because she felt it was a little way of God saying that He had been looking after her.

At the time, she'd been a little annoyed because there was so little room in her trailer, she couldn't even hide Christmas gifts. But it had turned out to be a good thing.

Maybe not the best thing that could ever happen, but a good thing, nonetheless.

She found the tarp in the shed without too much trouble and was able to close the doors a lot easier than she opened them, all the while thinking about how she was going to keep the cold air out and whether or not they could continue to live in the trailer when part of it had collapsed.

There would be some insurance on it, but she'd been told when she got the policy that her trailer wasn't worth much and most likely if any kind of major catastrophe happened, the insurance company would consider it totaled and just give her the current value.

Which wasn't much.

Her phone buzzed in her pocket as she walked to the house, and she remembered that she'd never texted Keene back.

He would help you. If you let him.

She didn't want to. She didn't want him to have to keep coming to her rescue. She wanted to be able to handle this on her own or have someone else other than Keene help her. She didn't want to appear to him like a helpless, pathetic woman who couldn't hold anything together. She was tired of looking weak and incapable. Poor and underprivileged.

She wanted to be strong. Tough. Able to handle things on her own.

But it would be nice to have someone to lean on.

Chapter 15

If Shelby had a husband, she would be leaning on him.

But she couldn't lean on Keene. He was quickly becoming a friend, but nothing more.

He'd already done so much for her...and the thought occurred to her that was all in vain as well. What good would an addition do when the trailer was totaled?

Still, she needed to answer him, or he might get worried and feel like he needed to stop in, so she set the tarp down on the steps, pulled off her gloves, and pulled her phone out.

Sure enough, the latest text was from him as well.

I'm coming in. I'll stop around and check on you. If you don't want me to bother you, just say so.

He didn't seem angry in the text. At least, she didn't read it like anger, but maybe he was thinking her lack of response meant she wasn't interested. Or she didn't want him around.

That wasn't true. Not in the slightest.

Her thumbs flew over the screen quickly.

Sorry. Had a few unexpected things happen. Thank you for checking on me. I got home just fine.

She sent the text and then realized she'd never answered about him coming in.

So she wrote another one.

You don't need to stop. Thank you anyway.

Her hand hovered over the send button. Should she? She wasn't really lying. Actually, not at all. She was just answering his question, telling him he didn't need to come. That was the truth. She didn't need him.

Maybe she wanted him. Maybe she longed with all her heart to have someone with her while she handled this, but she didn't need him. She had the Lord.

That was all she needed, right?

And the Lord gave you friends. Why would you turn down a friend's offer of help? Especially when you need it.

Man, she hated it when that little voice in her head made all kinds of sense.

She hit the delete button and erased that message.

Before she could write anything else, a text from him came in.

How's your mother? I can watch the kids while you sleep if she's not well. I'll also shovel your drive. I'm doing it for Miss Ginny anyway.

She stared at her phone. Not noticing how the cold numbed her fingers and the snowflakes fell and melted on the screen. Uncertain whether the heaviness in her chest was relief or guilt or fear or just her sense of not being good enough.

She hadn't done anything to make this man want to help her. She wasn't anything that should turn his head or catch his eye. And yet... He didn't just want to take her out and see if he could steal a kiss at the end of the evening or maybe more. He actually wanted to...help her.

Wasn't that what love was? She didn't really earn it. It wasn't something that was because of who you were or what you looked like. It was something you were given, and it didn't falter—even when you didn't deserve it.

Keene seemed to have that whole sacrificial love thing down. Where it didn't matter what people looked like or who they were or what they had; he loved them and was kind to them anyway.

I'll be up when you get here. Maybe we can talk then.

She sent it, not knowing what else to say. It would take too long to try to explain with her thumbs everything that had happened to her since she'd gotten home from work, from the roof to her mom to the kids, the peace she felt, the tarp, just...everything.

She had the tarp inside and put up and had used duct tape to seal the edges so that, while it wasn't insulated, it at least kept the snow out and the wind as well. They'd still burn through a lot more oil than they normally did, but she felt like her family would be okay and wouldn't freeze to death in the living room at least.

"Are you okay, Mom?" she asked, putting the roll of duct tape back in the cupboard where she kept it and turning to her mom.

"Sure. The kids seem happy to snuggle, and they're excited about how much snow we've gotten."

"I want to go out and play in the snow," Haley said.

"Let me get the roof shoveled off so that I don't accidentally hit you with snow coming off the roof, and then you can go out and play. We've got enough snow that I don't think you have to worry about this going anywhere before you get a chance to do all the playing your heart desires in it," she said, earning a big smile from Haley.

"And as soon as the room warms up a little, I'm going to need your help to cook breakfast anyway," her mom added, still snuggled down in the blanket on the couch.

Shelby went out, back to the shed, where the doors opened a lot easier than they had before despite the snow that had fallen in the meantime.

She had the shovel and the ladder and had made her way onto the roof when Keene's truck rumbled on the road.

Only a single snowplow had gone by since she'd been out, so the rumble definitely made her look up.

She wasn't the only one on their trailer shoveling the roof off, although as far as she could see, she was the only one whose roof had caved in.

Still, she recognized Keene's truck. The peace that was in her still wrapped around her heart, giving her a very real sense of calm. It was only shaken a little by the excited tripping of her heart.

It was silly for her to be excited to see Keene. She was trying to survive, and she definitely didn't have time for romance. But the tripping of her heart was very much like the tripping of a schoolgirl looking at the boy she found cute.

Shoving another section of snow off the roof, making sure to keep well away from the edge so she didn't slip off, she took a minute after the snow had dropped with a satisfying plop to watch Keene ease off the road beside her trailer lot, and she threw up her hand in a wave.

Figuring she could get another section or two shoveled off before he got out and made his way to the trailer—since he couldn't pull into their small parking area because she hadn't pulled her car the whole way up—she moved back and was in the process of doing that when she heard his voice.

"What are you doing up there? I can do that."

"But I thought it would be fun. I mean, come on, how often do you get to climb up on your roof and hang out?"

She laughed at herself. What was she doing being so carefree, almost goofing?

It was that peace. That confidence that no matter how much of a mess her life seemed, God had it. So she could smile and have a good time.

Grateful for the peace, she smiled, setting her shovel down on top of the roof and leaning on the handle.

"I think you're a little crazy, but I kinda like it," Keene finally said, his hands on his hips, his head tilted.

"You said it yesterday—what happens to us doesn't really matter, it's pleasing God and loving other people. I think God is more pleased when I'm happy than He is when I'm complaining." She shrugged her shoulders, and he shook his head.

"So, your roof has caved in at the front of the trailer, and you're up on the top of the back of the trailer, laughing, and making jokes, and... It didn't occur to you to maybe text me and let me know that, hey, your house caved in?"

"You're here. I didn't have to tell you. You just saw for yourself." Kinda funny, the more she let it go, the more unconcerned she was about it. Her words contained that easy, relaxed peace. And happiness like she'd never known before settled down in her soul. She felt like laughing.

"You're a nutcase. Certified." He laughed again. "Come on down from there. I'll finish that, then we'll figure something out with your roof."

"Why don't you come on up and help me? But I'm honestly having a lot of fun up here."

"If the lady insists," he said, sounding like he was giving up, but she heard the laughter in his voice. She should have known he had a shovel in the back of his truck, and he reached over and grabbed it before he climbed the ladder and onto the roof.

"Be careful. Where I've shoveled the snow off, it's extremely slippery."

"Thanks for the warning. I'm trying not to worry about you. But that didn't help."

"I think the person that worries is usually the one that ends up in the ER, so just watch your step, okay?" she threw over her shoulder, pushing the shovel into the next section of snow and using her abdomen along with her hands to shovel the heavy load toward the edge of the roof.

"At least it's not that far down, and with all the snow on the ground, the landing shouldn't be too hard."

"It actually hurts worse than you would think to fall into a pile of snow," she said, like he hadn't grown up in Iowa too.

"That's true, but freshly fallen snow isn't as bad as a heaping pile of frozen stuff."

"You sound like you have some experience with it."

"A little. At least I didn't dive headfirst into a frozen pile of stuff the way Preston did. I think that's what's wrong with him."

"Oh my goodness. I bet that hurt."

"Yeah, the thing I remember the most about it was the blood everywhere. It looks really red against white snow. He split his forehead open as well as his lip and broke his nose. He was a mess for a while."

"I don't think my girls will ever do that to me, but I suppose I should keep my eye on Perry."

"Maybe with two older sisters, he'll have a bit more common sense. It seems to be something boys with no girls in the family lack."

"I'll keep that in mind. Maybe that's something else boys with no sisters are missing—someone to pull them back from the edge and tell them how dumb they're being."

"I wonder why we're having a little bit of role reversal. Have you noticed that?"

"I'm not getting too close to the edge."

"You're up here. That's enough."

"And is it any different if I'm up here rather than you?"

"Will you get mad at me if I say yes?"

"Of course, not. If you can back it up with facts."

"Men were made to shovel off roofs. Women were made to be inside and make the man the soup that she'd promised days ago and he's still waiting for."

"Okay. That's not fair."

"How so? Facts, right?"

"Well, you might be pushing it a bit on the homemade stuff."

"I don't know. This feels like it's a man's job. It seems like common sense says this is the man's job. But if you want to admit to liking it, I'm not going to argue with you about it."

"That's about a sideways argument if I ever heard one. There are no facts, so you're just gonna make something up."

"Hey. It worked. I distracted you from the argument, and you can't even remember what we were arguing about anymore."

"I can." She grunted at the extra heavy load of snow on her shovel. "But it seems kind of pointless to beat a dead horse. You can just say I won."

"The lady wants me to lie now." He shook his head, shoveling a lot easier than she was, and she tried not to stare, admiring.

"No. I just wanted you to admit when you've lost. I know. It's hard."

"I can admit when I've lost, and it is possible there are some things around here that I have lost, but this argument isn't one of them." He huffed a laugh along with a grunt as another load of snow fell off the roof.

She pushed hers off, too, before asking, "Did you already clear off Miss Ginny's walk?"

"No. I came here first." He seemed very interested in the snow he was shoveling, and he didn't look at her while he spoke. "I might have been a little concerned about you."

"I would say the concern was unfounded, but I am missing some of my roof, so maybe you're more intuitive than you look."

"Maybe." He didn't say anything more although she kinda felt like there was something he would have added, except...maybe he felt uncomfortable.

They just had a little more to do, and they finished in silence, shoving off the rest of the snow, and then he offered her his hand, saying, "Let me help you back to the ladder. You're right about it being slippery, and I think you're going to have a pretty busy day even without a trip to the ER."

She looked at his hand, no gloves, calloused and hard. One that was reaching out to her, to help with no strings. No expectations.

How many times had she been with a man and not felt like he wasn't expecting at least something in return for whatever he was doing? Even if she didn't give it to him, the expectation still felt real.

She put her gloved hand in his and looked up into his eyes.

"Thank you." They stood there like that, her throat tight, her heart full. The peace that she'd been feeling ever since her roof had caved in still completely enveloped her, but her heart kicked up just that much and encouraged her to take a chance. On what, she wasn't sure, maybe just on letting go and not worrying.

Appreciating what was, not trying to figure out what could be.

"My pleasure," he finally murmured. His voice didn't sound altogether steady either. Almost as one, they turned, their gazes moving away, and they walked toward the ladder, with him helping her to the edge and steadying her as she put first one leg over then the other. He tossed her shovel down into the snow and then his along beside it, then he followed her down when she was safely on the ground.

"I'm sorry I don't have any soup ready for you, but you're welcome to come in for a bit."

"You haven't slept since yesterday afternoon. You don't have to apologize for not having soup. And if you don't mind, I would like to come in, would like to talk to you about what you're going to do about your roof." He put a hand up. "I know it's none of my business. But are we good enough friends that I can have a little bit of say or at least offer suggestions as to what I think you should do?"

"We are. We definitely are. You've been better to me than some of my lifelong friends. And for no reason."

"Maybe you just inspire that kind of loyalty. That's a reason."

"Then it's only in you. Because I don't see anyone else around here dying to be loyal and offer friendship to me."

"Maybe you should stop looking a gift horse in the mouth and just accept the fact that I like you. And I consider you a friend. And that means I do things like check up on you, and worry about you, and shovel off your roof, and care about you and your kids and your mom and what's going to happen to you when your roof caves in. Does that make sense?" he asked, a grin tugging at the corners of his lips, like he knew it didn't. Not really.

Her lips followed his up, almost like she couldn't help it, and she shook her head. "What is, is, and I'm just gonna be happy about it."

"I like it. Let me put my shovel in the back of my truck, and I'll be in."

Chapter 16

Keene couldn't believe that Shelby's roof had caved in and her text had not been a panicked plea for help.

He kind of wanted to get offended over it, but he understood that it was tough to ask for help. Especially when a person already felt like they were down. Maybe being the youngest in a bunch of brothers had taught him that; through most of his childhood he'd almost always rather tried get himself out of a scrape than ask for his brothers' help.

He'd outgrown that now, but he remembered Shelby from high school. She'd been pretty and popular, and everything had come easily to her. She wasn't used to asking for help and needing it, and she'd been pretty open about the fact that she felt like it was her poor choices that had led her to where she was anyway.

So he didn't take it personally, the fact that she hadn't asked for his help, and figured it wasn't him, it was the fact that she hated that she had already needed so much, and it was mostly her pride.

Pride was a bad thing when it made you think of yourself more highly than you ought. But it could also inspire a person to get themselves out of a bad situation, so he couldn't discount it entirely.

Still, when he'd realized her roof had caved in, he'd expected to see her all worried and upset.

He hadn't expected to hear her joking about it.

He suspected that he'd been falling for her. A week ago, he would have said that someone couldn't fall in love so quickly.

Now, he supposed experience was a great mind changer.

Striding up the steps, smiling at the irony that he'd fixed them just in time for the roof to cave in, he rapped on the door, then opened it, figuring she knew he was coming in and not wanting to make her stop whatever she was doing to have to open the door.

He knocked his boots against the step, removing most of the snow off of them before he stepped in, but when he walked in, he stayed on the rug and stamped a couple of times to get the rest of the snow off.

Miss Cindy was at the stove, Haley and Grace on either side of her, and she looked over her shoulder when he stepped in.

"Good morning. I think I remember seeing you Friday at the school."

"You look a little better than you did then. Feeling better?"

She nodded. "Sometimes it lasts a while, but thankfully, I'm not quite as exhausted as I sometimes am. Although, there's still pain."

"I guess that's something you have to learn to live with."

She nodded and turned back to the stove while Grace and Haley made their way across the kitchen and both of them stood on either side of him with their arms around his waist.

While he chatted with them about their parts in the play yesterday and their excitement at getting to go out in the snow and play, he racked his brain trying to figure out what he could do to help Shelby.

The insurance probably wasn't going to give them much for the roof. Probably not enough to fix it. The trailer most likely wasn't worth the cost.

He could donate the material and fix it himself. And if he worked hard, he could probably have it done in a day or two.

His brothers might even help him although none of them were the carpenters he was, but with some help, he might even get it done sooner.

But another idea had been floating around in the back of his head, and he kind of wanted to do that.

The girls left his side to help their gram put breakfast on the table, and Shelby came out from where she had changed into dry clothes.

They invited him to sit down, and while he wanted to solve the problem immediately, he hadn't eaten before he'd gotten up and done the barn work that morning. Then he'd come right in after he was finished, so he was hungry.

He sat down, chatting about nothing and anything with the girls and Miss Cindy while Shelby was a little quieter than normal but seemed exceptionally calm, and there was almost a glow of happiness about her that he couldn't really explain.

It was attractive. He couldn't deny it.

Finally, breakfast ended and the girls got dressed and went outside to play while Miss Cindy sat in the living room and Perry played with trucks on the floor.

Keene carried a load of dishes from the table while Shelby stood at the dishwasher loading it.

"It bothers me that you haven't slept since yesterday."

"The convenience store is closed. They told me when they called in and said that I should lock up after I left that they probably wouldn't open until at least tomorrow. Possibly the day after tomorrow. As long as we can find a place to sleep tonight, I'm going to get rest. A good night's sleep."

"About that," he said immediately, knowing this was the perfect opportunity. "I can probably fix your roof although I think it's going to cost more than what your trailer is worth. Assuming you have insurance?"

She nodded. He loved that she wasn't giving him a hard time for putting his nose in where it probably didn't belong.

"I do. But I think you're right."

"Regardless, I can make sure we get the materials and get it fixed irrespective of whether the insurance covers it, but I had a different idea."

"You did?"

"Yeah. Please don't you take it wrong. I'm not suggesting anything inappropriate. But Braxton just moved out of the farmhouse and Preston's been helping Gram. Elias hasn't lived there for a while, so it's just me."

He had been in the process of wringing the rag out to go wipe the table, but he paused, leaning against the island on the opposite side of the dishwasher and waiting until she looked up at him.

"You can move in there. I can charge rent if that makes you feel better. But there's plenty of bedrooms for everyone, including you and your mom and all three kids. I am... I don't know that you want it to be a long-term solution. I don't want people to think there's anything inappropriate going on, but that would solve your problems. And if you wanted to help with the chicken barn, I would pay you. And you could quit one of your jobs. You wouldn't have to leave the farm to work, and...it just might be better all around."

Maybe he should have given her an opportunity to think about it before he laid it all on her. Broken it to her gently, in small pieces, because she slowly straightened, a dirty glass in her hand, a plate in the other one, and stared at him.

A little smile playing around her lips.

Finally, after what felt like an eternity, where the only sounds were Perry's truck noises from the living room and the occasional murmur of Miss Cindy as she talked to him, Shelby spoke.

"I know. I'm supposed to politely decline. Tell you it's too much. Protest that you shouldn't go out of your way for me, but...I'm not gonna do any of that." She huffed out a breath. "I haven't been worried about what was going to happen. I figured God would provide a solution. And while you were speaking, although my pride kind of rebelled against what you are saying, the peace that I've been feeling all day just warmed and shimmered inside of me. I don't know how else to explain it. And it just feels like the perfect solution. Are you sure?" She seemed to have to add on that last part, like she just couldn't help herself.

"Yeah. I didn't even want to suggest fixing the roof because I would rather move you and your kids into my house. But I didn't want you to think that that was the only solution. I'm sure there are others too. We could talk to the pastor, and there might be a family willing to take you all in. Maybe an older lady like Miss Ginny."

"I love the idea of my kids being on a farm. I just... I don't want to put you out. We're loud and noisy and messy. I'm not always this happy. And I really don't have anything. Nothing except bills and a big, happy, messy family."

"I'm no stranger to bills. I'm a farmer, remember? And I've kind of been longing for a happy, messy family."

He hadn't really meant to say that last line, but it seemed to slip out, and he let it go. Letting the words hang in the air while she stared at him.

"Well, I'm trying to work on my bills. I have a complaint open with the credit card company, but so far, it's taking a really long time for them to do their investigation or whatever it was they said they were doing. And when I consulted a lawyer, he suggested that until they were finished, I needed to just work on paying it, which was the best thing for me and my credit."

"I get it."

"I just... I want to pay rent, but I'm afraid I can't afford the amount that I should, the amount that what you're offering me is worth."

"You're going to keep me from being lonely in that big old house. That's worth something. You can decorate it too, and that's worth something as well. And it'll be like having a family there, which is worth more than money."

"I think you're a little crazy," she said with a laugh.

"I think that makes two of us." The words he'd said to her while she'd been standing on the roof kinda hung in the air between them, and they smiled together. It was a smile of communication and understanding and shared humor, an intimate smile, the kind of smile that people who knew each other and liked each other and wanted to be with each other smiled to each other.

The kind of smile that she hadn't smiled too many times in her life.

It was good.

Chapter 17

"So it's settled?" Keene said gently, almost as though he hadn't wanted to break the spell between them but he was prompted by something, maybe the fact that he wanted Shelby to sleep. And she honestly was kind of feeling it now. After being up so long, and the physical exertion, and the cold air, she did feel a little bit like a collapse was imminent.

"It's settled. I'm not sure how good I'm going to be at packing right now, though. Suddenly I just feel extremely tired."

"How about we just grab some overnight clothes, and we'll head out to the farm. We'll pack later. I don't want to push." His eyes seemed to get a little more intense as he leaned toward her. "But I'm assuming that you're going to quit at least one of your jobs and you'll have a little more time? Packing and moving isn't easy. I don't want you to do more than what you're able to. Having you get sick—or drop from exhaustion—isn't going to benefit anyone. Although, I'll make sure you're taken care of."

He said the last part with a special emphasis, like that would ease her mind.

In one sense, it did, but in another sense, she didn't want to be a burden.

"I don't want you to have to take care of me. I'm not a two-year-old, and I'm not eighty. I'm an able-bodied woman, and I should be able to take care of myself and my children."

"You don't have to do it all. I'm here to help."

"You might be taking the friendship thing a little bit too far. I appreciate your help. Truly I do. But...it makes me uneasy because our relationship is so lopsided. All you're doing is helping me, and...I don't have anything to give in return. Do you understand how that makes me feel?"

"Maybe you're giving me the satisfaction of being able to help someone I really like?" He emphasized the fact that he liked her. He lifted his shoulder and stepped back. "Maybe I've been lonely. Maybe you're doing more for me than what you realize."

She had thought there wasn't any kind of ulterior motive involved in what he was doing. Truly she hadn't, but his words seemed to underscore that and make her realize that he was serious. He really thought that he was getting as much out of it as she was. Maybe just not in the ways she wanted him to.

"It's a great offer, and I would be a fool to turn it down. I just don't know how to thank you."

"Quit one of your jobs. Take it easy for a little bit. Have fun with your kids. That will be thanks enough."

"Does an old lady get a little say in this?"

Shelby startled and tore her eyes away from Keene toward where her mother stood at the edge of the counter. She hadn't even heard her come over.

"Of course," she said, her breath still a little puffy from the scare.

"I'd love to hear your opinion," Keene said casually. Relaxed. Although, surely he hadn't been any more aware of her mother standing there than she had.

"I know people do this all the time. And I'm not knocking them. They can do whatever they want. But, Shelby, do you really want to do what is essentially living with a man to whom you're not married?"

Shelby's eyes grew wide, and she pulled her lip in. She hadn't thought about it like that. And even though she knew all the arguments—they wouldn't be sharing a room, she would be renting from him, it wasn't like that at all, she needed a place to stay—she knew her mom was probably right.

If she wanted to avoid all appearance of evil, as the Bible commanded, it might not be such a great idea.

"Miss Cindy, I could move her out there and then come back in here and stay in town. Possibly with Miss Ginny or Gram? Would that be okay?" Keene's voice was still level, reasonable, conversational. She hadn't upset him with her accusation, and he wasn't desperately grasping at straws to keep her out there.

"Oh no." Shelby shook her head. "I couldn't allow that. It's one thing for us to move in with you. It's a completely different thing for us to move in and you to move out. That's ridiculous."

"That would be different. And I would be okay with that," her mother said thoughtfully.

"I wouldn't want to do anything that would offend you, Miss Cindy. Or cause you to be upset with your daughter or lose respect for me."

"I have a high amount of respect for you, son. Your reaction just now is probably one of the main reasons why."

"I don't want to lose that."

Shelby looked between them, wanting to throw her hands in the air. "That's really nice. I'm glad she respects you, and I'm glad you appreciate it, but it's a little bit ridiculous. You admitted yourself people do it all the time, Mom."

"But she's right. Christians should be different. We shouldn't just fall in with what the rest of the world does and be okay with it."

"That's kind of judgmental," she said irritably, falling back on the old argument that everyone used.

"I'm not judging anyone if they want to do that. That's fine. They get to stand before the Lord and talk to Him about it for themselves. But as for us, I want to do what's right. I want to avoid any appearance of evil. I don't want to give anyone else a cause for stumbling, where they might point at us and say, 'hey, they did it, why can't we?' Or maybe we'd just make it a little easier for someone else. Even though we're not really sinning." He lifted his shoulder. "It makes sense to me."

"You can't move out," she said with finality. She was not going to displace him from his home. "Maybe I could find somewhere else we could stay, or...I don't know..." Her voice kind of faded off.

She had been so hopeful this was going to work out. So grateful that she might even be able to quit her job. Why did her mom have to go and throw the religious argument into the mix?

But even as she thought that, she was glad her mother had. As much as she loved that it would have been a great solution, she wanted to be a good example for her children.

"Miss Cindy?"

"Yes, son?"

When had her mom started calling Keene son?

"What if I married her? Would it be okay then?"

Her mother didn't hesitate. "Yes."

"Mom! I barely know him!"

"You've known him all your life. You went to school with him. You know his family. And he knows you."

"But... But I haven't fallen in love with him." She wasn't entirely sure that was true, but it was the only thing she could think of to say. And she didn't understand why he wasn't protesting, except... He'd suggested it!

"A good marriage consists of more than lovey-dovey feelings. I would think after the marriage that you were in, you would know that."

Man, she hated when her mom was reasonable. Especially when she was reasonable for the opposite argument as the side she was on.

"That's true," she said, much more subdued than she had been.

"Shelby hasn't slept since yesterday, and time is ticking by. She has to be exhausted. How about we gather some overnight clothes, I'll take you all out to the farm, and I might stay, especially until the work is done, but I'll come back in here and stay somewhere for this evening. Will that work for you, Miss Cindy?"

"It will. And I appreciate it." She nodded her head, gave Shelby a look, and turned. But then she turned back. "I guess... I guess all my clothes are in my room. I suppose I'll be okay just wearing these."

"If you tell me where they are, I'll grab you some. Plus, I think I'd better shut off the water and drain all the spigots because it's likely to freeze. Maybe we should also turn the electricity off and get things closed up so that it's okay to leave this overnight. Or even for a couple of days."

"That sounds good." Her mom went back over to the couch and eased herself down on it while Shelby stood in the kitchen, drumming her fingers on the counter, agitated, but also...realizing that the peace she had was still there. Maybe stronger.

Her mom was right. Marriage to Keene wouldn't exactly be a risk. And she could fall in love with him easily. But part of her felt like maybe he'd be getting the short end of the stick. And she'd already been feeling like that a lot. She didn't want to add to it.

"Why don't you let it go? Just let it rest in your head. And we'll do what we said we're gonna do, and tomorrow when you wake up, maybe things will be clearer for you."

She looked over at him, unruffled and not the slightest bit concerned. In fact, if anything, he looked a little amused.

"What are you smiling at?" she said, a little irritation leaking into her voice although his smile made hers turn up as well.

"I think your mom likes me."

Chapter 18

Keeping his word, Keene took Shelby and her children to his farm, along with her mother. He helped them unload and settle in before he did the evening work, using the tractor to clear the long driveway and making sure before he left that everything was working in the barn for the night. When he checked the house again and said good night to everyone, Shelby was already in bed. Glad she was getting some sleep, he drove back into town.

He'd already texted Preston who was taking care of Gram and was totally fine with Keene coming for the night.

Gram had plenty of bedrooms upstairs; he'd just have to make his own bed. Preston had thrown sheets in the laundry for him, and they would be dry when he got there.

It wasn't very late, just a little after eight, so it didn't surprise him that Preston was still up.

Gram was in the living room sleeping on a chair, and Preston sat in the recliner beside her.

Keene walked in the kitchen, taking his boots off and setting them where the snow would melt and not make a big puddle of muddy water on the floor.

Padding on stockinged feet through the kitchen, he thought he might make it through the living room, but Preston looked up from where he was writing in a book.

"Going through without saying anything?"

"I didn't want to bother Gram."

"She doesn't have her hearing aid in. You won't bother her."

"I see. I saw the sidewalks were cleared off. You were busy today."

"Yeah. I was actually having fun. I did Gram's and pretty much everyone's on the block. And stopped by Miss Ginny's like you asked me to. I could have made a lot of money if I hadn't turned it all down."

"Maybe you should pay Gram for the use of her snowblower. Because I'm pretty sure you weren't doing all that with a shovel."

Preston snorted. "You're just jealous because you weren't using it."

"I'm not gonna deny that. I didn't wish I was staying with Gram, but close maybe."

"It wasn't even close. You'd much rather be hanging out with Shelby than Gram. I saw you guys at the school play. You looked pretty enamored. I actually had a bet going on with Braxton to say that you'd be asking me to take your date home so you could go home with Shelby. I lost, by the way."

"I never thought of that—getting you to take Lacey home. That was a really good idea. You should have said something to me. I could have made sure you won that bet if you'd have agreed to split your winnings."

They laughed, but then Preston sobered. "How long is she staying out on the farm?"

"I'm not sure," Keene hedged. He hadn't really wanted to go into everything with his brother, but...Preston had a good head on his shoulders, and he'd give him biblical counsel. Maybe he should talk about it with someone rather than just thinking that the idea was good just because he liked it. "I asked her to marry me."

"What?"

"That's right. I asked her to marry me."

"Just because she's staying on the farm for a couple of days?"

"It could be longer than a couple of days. Her roof caved in. And while everything else looks okay and I can get lumber and fix it, it just seems like it might make more sense to use that as a springboard for going in a different direction."

"Marriage is a pretty serious direction."

"That's why I'm telling you about it."

"How about you explain exactly what's going on before I give you my opinion? I can hardly do that without all the facts."

Keene briefly explained what had gone on and how Miss Cindy had objected and the solution he'd offered.

"Well," Preston said, closing his book and setting it on the coffee table beside him. He pushed the recliner down and leaned forward, resting his elbows on his knees, his expression serious. "It sounds to me like it might not be something that you get to decide since the lady's not sure she's going to take you."

"That's true. She could say no." He didn't like the way that idea made him feel. Like his stomach was sick and his heart was beating through thick gunk.

"I'm not sure there's anything for me to say," Preston finally said, lifting his head and looking his brother in the eye.

Keene met his gaze. He hadn't done anything wrong. In fact, he felt like he was trying to do things as right as he could.

"Do you think maybe I was too hasty in offering marriage? It's not the way normal people start a traditional marriage, but anyone who's working the way she is has the kind of character that I want in my wife. And it's true, I haven't been around her much, but she's funny and fun and she's trying to do right. I think, as long as she's willing to commit, I can trust her to keep her vows. I can also depend on her to want to do right in our marriage. I guess... I guess I just don't see how I could want anything else, you know?"

"What if some girl comes along that you fall in love with? You can't do anything because you're stuck with Shelby."

"I guess I don't see it as being stuck with her. I see it as getting to be with her. I just haven't spent one single second with her that hasn't been fun. Or...it's not that I think marriage has to be fun, but you do want to enjoy the person you're married to, right? You don't want to be married to someone who's going to complain all the time. Or be lazy. Or expect you to do all the heavy lifting. And she doesn't. She expects to pull her own weight. And she takes care of her children. They're her priority. I love that. It shows she's not selfish. Or at least not as selfish as she could be."

"I see. It sounds like maybe you thought about this."

"I have. Prayed about it. But you know how when you really want something, all of a sudden you're sure it's God's will. I got to thinking that maybe you could show me where my logic is wrong at least."

"It doesn't line up with what the rest of the world thinks. There's that."

"When have we ever been concerned about that? I mean, come on, we don't really do anything the way the rest of the world does, ever, right?"

"I know. But people get funny. They'll say you didn't know her long enough. That it's never going to last. Sometimes it's hard to fight the tide, you know?"

"I know. All their negativity convinces you that you're wrong. And you cave even when you know you shouldn't. Maybe that's what I'm looking for. Confirmation that I'm doing God's will. And it's not just what I want."

"I really can't give you that. God isn't going to show me His will for you. But I like your reasoning. You aren't spouting some pie-in-the-sky, I'm madly in love with her, we have to get married fast because I don't want to lose her reason. It sounded to me like you're getting married for the right reasons. Commitment, character, willingness to grow and to do right. That's what makes a good marriage."

"That's what I was thinking."

"Now you just need to talk to her."

"I know. That's gonna be hard. Because I love her kids, but it's hard to have an adult conversation with them around. And she works so much..."

"Gram's doing really well. Tell me when Shelby will be free and will-ing to talk to you, and I'll take the kids and Miss Cindy. We'll get some ice cream, come here, and visit Gram for a bit. That'll give you an hour, maybe two. That enough time?"

Keene looked at his older brother. He'd heard the rumors. Knew them to be probably true. That Preston had fallen in love with Carmen in high school. Something had happened, Keene didn't know what, and Carmen had married someone else. That Preston had never stopped loving her.

But as far as he knew, Preston hadn't talked to her, wasn't around her, didn't stalk her, and had never tried to break up their marriage or steal her out from underneath her husband's nose.

Preston would never do such a thing. He was a man who was upright and honest. He wanted to do right, and even if his heart was broken, even if it meant he would be miserable, even if it meant he would never be happily married with a family of his own, he would never step into someone else's marriage.

Keene had to admire that.

"I'd appreciate that," he finally said, wishing there was something he could do to help his brother. He supposed, though, if Preston still was in love with Carmen after all these years, introducing him to someone else wouldn't help. Nothing would. And Keene wouldn't want Preston to not be a one-woman man because there was something to be said about a man who was faithful. Was there any better thing? That a man be found faithful?

Chapter 19

Carmen Davis wiped her hands on the towel at the back of the fast-food restaurant where she worked and hung it back on the rack.

"I'll take the garbage out before I go on break. Be back in fifteen," she said to Kelly, her coworker and manager on the shift.

"That's fine. I'll sign you out in five," Kelly said distractedly, her eyes glued to the monitor, watching the order that was coming in.

Carmen was making a little more than minimum wage, and on some shifts, she was the shift manager. But when she got daylight, Kelly still outranked her.

Which was fine. She still preferred daylight because then she was home when her children were.

With the snowstorm, she'd appreciated a few days off, but school was open again and it was back to the old grind.

Although, everything had been made harder because of the snow and the arctic cold front that had come through after, turning everything to ice and making life just that much more of a struggle.

But that was Iowa, and that, along with the wind that never stopped, was part of the privilege of living in wide-open spaces and being the breadbasket of the country.

Shoving her hat down on her head but forgoing her coat, she shoved the door open. It would be nice to cool down for a little bit, and by the time she was cold, her break would be over. She probably wouldn't even need a watch.

Lifting the top of the big garbage can just outside the door, she pulled. Usually they popped right out, but this one was heavy, like someone had thrown a bunch of full drinks away or maybe a cement block or something.

She tugged again, and the black bag started to come up slowly. Maybe it was frozen to the bottom and she'd be able to grab it once it unstuck.

But no such luck; the bag came out slowly. Not bothering to try to figure out why it was so heavy, she tied it off at the top, grabbed the extra bag that she'd shoved in her pocket previously, and put it in, replacing the top.

The dumpsters were inconveniently located across the parking lot in a fenced-in area, so she waited while a car pulled around going through the drive-through and another one pulled into a parking spot before she picked the bag back up and started lugging it across the icy blacktop.

A tall man got out of the car that had just parked and then opened the back door and worked on getting one of his kids out of a booster seat while two little girls hurried around the edge of his truck.

Carmen smiled. Men who took care of their children were always so appealing to her. On a purely surface level, since she was married, but since her husband had never helped her with her children or even seemed particularly interested in them, she especially appreciated a man who loved his children and wasn't afraid to spend time with them.

Maybe he was giving his wife the night off, or maybe he was divorced. Many people were nowadays.

She'd chosen to stay in her marriage, and she knew people talked badly about her because of it. That talk hurt her heart, but it didn't undermine her determination to keep her vows.

Just because other people had chosen differently didn't make them wrong. But it didn't make her wrong to decide to stay. To not see leaving justified in the Bible, and to want to do things God's way. Even if it was the hard way.

Maybe she had her head in the clouds, thinking about her marriage, or maybe the gust of wind would have blown her off course anyway, but she hit an icy patch just as an extremely strong gust of wind whipped down through the parking lot, making her slide on the ice, and that, along with the awkward and heavy bag of garbage, knocked her totally off balance.

By that time, the man and his kids were coming across the parking lot, and she just caught a glimpse of him as her arm swung wildly in the air and her feet sought for purchase, making her slide faster rather than helping her balance situation.

She slipped off the patch of ice, hit the blacktop, gripped immediately, and her leg stopped, while her upper body and the garbage bag did not. She plunged forward, and the bag hit the blacktop and broke, popping apart with garbage flying everywhere as she landed half on top of it and half on the hard parking lot surface.

Hopefully, anyone pulling in wouldn't run over her.

Pain shot up her arm, down her side, but the kind of pain that was from a scrape, where probably the blacktop had torn a hole in the long-sleeved T-shirt that she wore underneath her uniform.

Not the kind of pain that signaled a broken bone.

The older she got, the more pain she felt, so it wasn't too hard to clench her teeth, give herself a couple of seconds, then push to her knees.

By then, the man and his kids had stopped going toward the store, changing direction and moving toward her.

"Miss? Are you okay?" His voice had deepened over the years, but she still recognized the voice as Preston's.

Somehow, she'd recognize him anywhere. And that sweet sound lapped at her heart and curled her stomach, and her chest tightened at the sound of his voice like it always had, too.

"I'm fine," she said, keeping her head down, hoping he wouldn't recognize her. She just wanted him to leave so she wouldn't have to look at him. Wouldn't have to remember what she'd done, her stupidity, and what she had been living with ever since.

He'd never gotten married, but she could hardly believe it was because of her. Couldn't believe he would be pining over her.

Maybe it was because she'd given all women a sour taste in his mouth, and she couldn't blame him for that.

"Carmen?" he said, like he'd recognize her voice anywhere too.

"Yeah," she said, pulling out the second garbage bag that she'd shoved in her pocket. Two had come out when she'd pulled the one, and she'd shoved them both in her pocket. Thankfully, since she needed it now.

Shaking it open, she didn't look up but started picking up the garbage that had burst from the bag.

"Girls. Watch the ice, but let's help this lady get her garbage picked up."

This lady. She wouldn't use her name with his children. Preston wasn't married. They must be someone else's kids.

She wouldn't ask. She would act like she would with any other man, except Preston wasn't any other man.

"That was quite a fall. Are you sure you're okay?" Preston asked, and she glanced up. He was picking up trash with one hand while holding a young boy in the other.

"I'm fine," she said and looked away. Her husband was gone, on the road, and would be gone for several more days at least although he usually didn't tell her exactly when he was going to get home. Whether he didn't know, or whether he didn't want her to know or just didn't care enough to tell her, she wasn't sure.

Not that it mattered. She just knew, because of the type of relationship she was in, she was susceptible. Susceptible to someone who was kind to her, who cared about her, who would talk to her.

She knew, if she let her guard down, she could be tempted away. Because all the things she'd hoped for when she'd gotten married—the companionship, friendship, the affection, the whispered secrets and smiles, the journey together, laughter, fun, and even hardships made lighter because they shared them—none of that happened.

It had been all her all the time. A single mom who did a man's laundry and had a man visit once in a while. Who shared her paycheck and watched it disappear for cars and parts and whatever else took his fancy.

Someone like Preston could tempt her to abandon her values and the vows she struggled, even on a good day, to keep, so she kept her head down and didn't ask about the children. Didn't try to make small talk and risked coming off as rude. Being rude was better than seeing what she was missing and being tempted away.

Because she'd chosen this road, and she would walk it. No matter what.

Maybe Preston got the hint, or maybe he just couldn't think of anything else to say, but he put the garbage in the new bag quietly, all the while looking behind him as though watching for cars and protecting the children in his care.

She admired that.

Wished she'd had it for her own children. But it was only her standing between them and the things that could hurt them.

As the last piece of loose garbage got picked up and she was tying the garbage bag together at the top, he stood.

Just standing, not moving, as the girls gathered around him, while Carmen tied her bag together.

Finally, she couldn't fiddle around with it anymore, and she straightened herself—the bag that they'd picked up in one hand, the bag that had broken in the other.

She braced herself and looked in his eyes. He gazed steadily down at her, his expression guarded. Hooded. Unemotional.

"Maybe when you go in, you should clean that cut. You're bleeding through your sleeve."

"I'm fine."

She would not cry. She would not allow the unfamiliarity of a man's concern for her welfare to bring her to tears. She would not do it.

Sticking her chin out, she took a breath. "Thank you for helping me."

She allowed the guarded look to fall from her face as she looked at each of the girls holding onto his legs.

That could have been her family. She wished it had been. She wished she would have been smarter. But she hadn't and she wasn't and it wasn't and she wouldn't regret it. Not much anyway.

Not while she was standing in front of the man that tugged at her heart and tempted her away from what she knew to be right more than anyone else in the world.

"Girls, it was so sweet of you guys to help me pick up the trash. Thank you so much."

They giggled although the younger one's giggle was certainly more carefree than the older one, who looked mature for her age.

They said, "You're welcome, ma'am."

Their manners made Carmen smile, so reminiscent of her children at that age.

"Take care of yourself," Preston said, and then low, so low she wasn't sure whether it was him or the wind, she heard, "Please."

Then he turned and was gone—walking into the store, while she turned and walked toward the enclosed dumpsters. Throwing the bags in, she walked around and entered the small, fenced area where employees went in the summer on break and where smokers were forced to go all winter.

No one was there now, and she sat down at the small table, putting her elbows on the top of it and taking her gloves off before she put her head in her hands, deflated.

She hadn't talked to him in years, had hardly seen him at all in that amount of time. Running into him just started all those old longings she didn't want and couldn't have in her marriage. It was adultery, just as sure as if she'd walked away with him, instead of away from him, if her mind wouldn't let go.

She prayed for strength, for peace and contentment and the ability to continue on the path that she had chosen.

Chapter 20

"I'm glad you had so many extra clothes lying around the house." Shelby tramped behind him down the narrow path that they'd shoveled from the house to the drive where the tractor was waiting on them. Running. They still had a couple of older tractors that didn't have cabs, but he had deliberately chosen the bigger tractor with the blade on for today.

Not just because Shelby would have a seat beside him and be comfortable but also because of the heater.

After the snow had gone through, the wind had kicked up, as often happened, and the temperatures had dropped.

He'd been busy yesterday in town helping to get people plowed out and had only been around the farm to take care of the chickens and come in and sit down for the soup that Shelby had cooked.

Her kids hadn't been kidding about it being really good. Unfortunately, there hadn't been any yeast in the house, though, so she hadn't made bread.

The next time he was in town, he'd fix that, and he was definitely hoping she'd do the whole soup and bread thing again.

Still, he'd left after supper, staying the night with Gram.

Two days had just solidified in his mind that he was making the right decision. It had been a spur-of-the-moment thing, but he felt a total peace about it and most definitely didn't want to take it back. If anything, he had to watch himself so that he wasn't pressuring Shelby to make the decision he wanted her to.

If they ended up together, he wanted it to be because she had decided on her own. Not because he pressured her. He didn't want her to have regrets.

Not that he thought that he would give her any chance at all to have regrets. He had every plan in the world of doing everything in his power to be the best husband and father he could.

But since he'd never done it before, he might make a terrible husband and father, and his best might be worse than what she was married to before.

Although, he doubted it. At least he didn't have any addictions that were going to bankrupt them.

"Okay. When you asked me to do this, I was excited about it. But now I'm nervous," she said from behind him as they walked around the dual wheels of the tractor.

"Nervous?" He looked over his shoulder, grinning. "Why would you be nervous? You think I'm going to wait until we're alone in the tractor together before I start becoming a completely different person?"

"No. I think I know better than that."

He couldn't walk beside her because the path was too narrow, but he smiled at that assurance that she seemed to trust him. Not that he'd ever given a reason not to. But after what she'd been through, she was understandably cautious about trusting people.

"Then, what?" he asked, putting his hand on the door latch and opening it.

"This is kind of big. And it's a little intimidating."

She stood beside him, looking up into the cab of the tractor and biting her lip.

"Don't feel like you have to. Because we can talk just as easily in the living room."

"That was so nice of Preston to take the kids out for lunch. He seems like such a nice guy."

"He's got a younger brother who is even nicer," Keene said, knowing that when Shelby said "nice guy," she wasn't really meaning "nicer than you"; although, she hadn't given him enough compliments for him to not have a little bit of jealousy over the kind words that she was throwing at his brother but hadn't given to him.

She's with you.

He knew it and tried to keep the petty jealousy, stemming from insecurity of what her feelings were, at bay.

"I'm kind of partial to his younger brother, honestly," Shelby said, looking up in the tractor again. "Even to the point where I'm going to get in this big scary thing and trust you to take care of me."

"Me? You're driving," he said, almost winking at her. But his grin allowed her to know that he was teasing her.

"Maybe in the summer when it's dry and there's no ice and we have a hundred-acre field that I can't run over anything in. Then I might consider driving something like this."

"It's just like a car. Only a little bigger."

"I'm not really that skilled at driving a car, so if you're thinking I won't be intimidated when you say it like that, you're wrong."

"Maybe it will ease your mind a little if I say that I've never actually wrecked the tractor although I've gotten several stuck. Does that help?"

"Stuck in snow?" she asked, one boot on the bottom step, one hand on the handle as she looked at him over her shoulder.

"No. Mud. And I was about twelve. I think I've learned a little bit since then anyway."

"That is reassuring. Because I assume every time it snows, you do this plowing."

She pulled herself up and stood beside her seat until he got up and went across her and sat down in his, pulling the door shut behind him.

"You comfortable?" he asked, knowing there wasn't really much he could do if she wasn't.

"I love the open feel of this. Too bad cars aren't surrounded by windows the way this is."

"The windows in here are definitely bigger."

"It's a huge difference." She was smiling, looking all around, and he enjoyed just watching her for a moment. He usually was very grateful for his job, that he got to be outside and work with constantly changing scenery. Even if the hours were long and the pay not that great and most of the time he had to do his own problem-solving.

"You didn't really answer my question. This is something that you usually do when it snows?" she asked again.

"That's right. The McCartney sisters live just to the west of us, and they usually do their own plowing, but when we get this much snow, I take our big tractor over and shove everything back for them. That way if we get more snow, there's a place to put it."

"I see. I remember the McCartney sisters from school, but it's been a long time since I've seen them."

"They spend a lot of time at the ranch. There are three of them, and they're pretty self-sufficient."

"And they never got married?"

"They took care of their parents for a while, and farming's a pretty hard job. They don't spend too much time off the farm, not because they don't want to, I don't think, but because there's always something that needs to be done. Although, one of them has been sick for a while, so the other two have been busy taking care of her on top of everything else. But if their farm is going to survive, they need to keep up with the work."

She nodded thoughtfully. "It's good for me to hear stuff like that. Because sometimes I think I'm struggling to make ends meet, working all the time and no time to do anything fun. But that's where a lot of people are. We just don't take the time to look and see and maybe lend a hand if we can."

He looked over to see her staring at him. He grinned, and she continued. "That's what I really admire about you. That you volunteered to help even though you're busy yourself and really don't have time."

"God says that the measure that we give will be what He measures to give back to us. And I don't think He's just talking about money. There are so many other things we can give beyond that. Although, I suppose that's probably the most appreciated at times."

"True, although what you're donating at the trailer, not just your time but your skill in building, I could never have done. It would have taken more money for me to hire someone to do what you volunteered to do if that makes sense."

"It does. But while you might consider it your job to take care of your children, that's still you giving of yourself. A lot of people don't."

"Don't...?"

"Don't take time for their children. Don't put them first. Don't make sure that they go to the Christmas play even though that means that they miss the sleep that they needed before they work the night shift."

He'd put the tractor in gear, going down the drive and just using the blade to shove the snow back a little further. He didn't have it down the whole way because he didn't want to scrape the stones off the drive, but it was always helpful to get the snow back, especially at the beginning of the season like this, in case they got more before it melted.

"Considering that you're living beside three unmarried ladies, it surprises me that you would..." She trailed off, as though embarrassed to finish her words or maybe not sure what to say.

He guessed, wanting to make things easier for her. "That I would be in town offering to marry you?"

"It does seem a little odd. I don't have anything. Other than three kids and a mom. I mean, come on. What kind of man in his right mind would look at me and be like, oh yeah, I want to hitch myself to her for the rest of my life?"

She put a hand up as though stopping him because he had opened his mouth to argue. "And don't get me wrong. I'm not putting myself down, necessarily, just being real. I mean a woman with three kids and a mom is not a man's fantasy. That's just a fact."

"Okay. I can give you that. You're right. The way a man doesn't necessarily hope to find a woman with three kids and a mom is the same way a woman doesn't necessarily hope to find a man who is romantically challenged, proposes marriage after knowing her for a week, and thinks the idea of a good time is driving around in a tractor together." He lifted a brow at her before slowing down as they came to the end of the drive, and he pulled out on the highway.

"Okay. That was a pretty good comeback," she said, nodding her head a little, sounding like she was thinking about it. "I guess we're agreeing that we're equally unappealing?"

He laughed. "Well, I didn't really answer your question. You're asking why I never dated any of the McCartney girls, and I guess that's because we grew up together. I mean, they're like sisters almost. We're not quite as close to them as we were to Bridget who neighbors us to the north, and they're all a little younger than we all are, but I don't know. They're just there. And it's kind of like I like them, and they're nice, and I consider them friends, but it's a little repulsive to think about dating them. Not in a bad way, just in a you wouldn't want to date your cousin kind of way. I guess."

"Okay. That was a pretty good explanation."

"Thanks, I think."

Maybe they were beating around the bush. Maybe he should just come right out and bring up the subject that he wanted to talk about. But maybe it was okay for them to just chat a little, get to know each other a bit.

Chapter 21

It didn't take Keene long to come up with something to talk about to make pleasant conversation. "I don't always appreciate the fact that I was able to grow up on a farm. Talk about playing with the McCartney girls, but my brothers and I did a lot of playing together too. In between a lot of hard work. It was a great life. You grew up in town. That had to be fun, too."

"It was. I guess. Although, I was an only child, so I didn't have the built-in playmates. And I didn't want to have an only child when I started having children. After growing up as one, I wanted a big family."

"Three kids is a big family?"

She laughed. "Well, maybe my plans got derailed a little because part of having a big family is having a parent team to take care of the kids. It's a lot harder if it's just one person."

"I can only imagine. Just getting the kids in the car is a chore. And that's just one job out of a lot that a parent has to do every day."

"Exactly. So I guess that kind of squashed my childhood dreams of having a big family. Although, kids take money too, and there wasn't a whole lot of that when I was having kids either."

"Yeah. That makes sense as well. Although, I think that's kinda changed over the years. Other than feeding them, which could be a pretty big expense, but back in the old days, they started being able to earn their keep, what? Around five or so? And 'their keep' was basically just helping to provide food for the family."

"It seems so simple. Hard, but simple. I'm not sure I could succeed if I had to grow and preserve all of my own food. If I couldn't go to the grocery store and pick something up, I would starve to death. I don't think about that too much, but it's scary if you do."

"I know. Maybe living out here, we thought about that a little bit more. Before we had the generator, the lights would go out, sometimes for days when I was a kid. And it was fun as a child, but it makes you think as you become an adult. What if something happens to the electric grid? There'd be a lot of people starving to death. Not right away. Of course. But within a year. For sure."

"So many of us don't even have the capability of attempting to grow food. I don't have any seeds. And I don't have any way of getting them if something were to happen to the electric grid. If our supply chain were interrupted. For example, if there was no fuel and trucks couldn't deliver groceries to the store. That's all it would take to create a national emergency where hundreds of thousands, even millions of people, would starve to death."

Her voice didn't have the confidence of someone who had thought about it for a long time, but more the wonder of someone who was just discovering the idea for the first time.

"That's a terrible thought," she mused.

"It is. I don't think that suffering like that is likely to happen. At least... I don't think. But there have been a lot of things that have happened that I never thought would have."

"That's true. Good things and bad things that have happened, things you thought maybe were impossible."

"Exactly. The kind of thing that bothers me is every time a bad thing happens, instead of looking to the Lord and then to our neighbors to help each other out, so many of us look to the government and want a solution there. It's almost like we replace God with government. And the government can't solve anyone's problems. Most of the time, anything the government gets involved in, they only make it worse."

She didn't jump in and agree with him, and he just kind of let his words hang there as he turned into the McCartney sisters' drive. They didn't have to agree on everything in order to be married, but his ideas didn't always line up with the rest of the world's, and maybe she didn't want to be married to someone whose drumbeat was so far away from what everyone else's was.

"So you don't think people should be involved in politics?" she asked, kind of like she was trying to figure out what exactly he had been saying.

"No. That's not really what I meant at all. I just meant if there was a problem—say a tornado or a hurricane, a snowstorm like this. Any kind of natural disaster. Used to be, we looked to God, and then we looked around to see who we could help." He shrugged, steering the tractor around a drainage ditch. "Now that we're taking God out of things, there's a void there, and the government steps in. And instead of being taught the basic Christian principle that it's important to help others and put yourself last, we assume the government's going to take care of it, and we don't put our nose in anyone else's business."

The farmhouse had come into view, but he figured he'd make another pass out the lane on both sides before he stopped to say anything to anyone.

"I see. So it's not politics you're against, it's... I guess government taking the place of God?"

"Yeah. I hate to say I'm against it, but it just seems like there's definitely a place for God in our lives, and when we take that out, we have to fill it with something."

"Like Jesus at Christmas. If you take Jesus out, you have to make Santa Claus bigger so he can fill in the gap."

"That's kind of the same thing. It's true for pretty much everything. When you take something out, you'll almost have to replace it with something. And oftentimes, the replacement is just a shady second from what the real thing is. Especially when we're talking about God."

"I hadn't thought about it like that before, but I can see that you're right. I can also see how that's very controversial and how people have almost been brainwashed into believing the exact opposite."

He shrugged. "I guess it doesn't matter. You're probably not going to stem the tide of the way the world is going. But you don't have to go blindly along with it. You can kind of look at it and see how maybe it would be better if they choose a different way."

He wasn't going to solve that problem. Nobody was.

God was big enough to, but He'd given man free choice. And Americans had been pretty clear about rejecting and replacing God.

"It amazes me, though, that someone would choose a government over God."

"Man's been doing that for thousands of years. Look at the Israelites rejecting God and demanding a king in Saul."

"Good point. But also, when you choose God, you know there are certain responsibilities that come with that. You have to give up your sin. Nobody wants to do that."

"True." She smiled a little, and he thought about him leaving the farm every night and sleeping somewhere else. It would be a lot easier to just stay on the farm and not worry about it. But a watered-down, easy version of Christianity wasn't much better than no Christianity at all.

"It's a lifestyle change. And we're comfortable where we are. We don't want to give up anything. We don't want to be uncomfortable. We're prideful, too, and don't want to be told we're wrong. We'll cling to our justifications that we've done the right thing and what we're doing is the right thing. It takes being uncomfortable and a certain humbleness and willingness to change in order to do things God's way."

"Some people convince themselves that that's not true."

"I agree. I've seen that. The Bible says that would happen. People have itching ears, they don't want to hear the truth, they want to hear whatever makes them happy."

"Exactly. So they twist the Bible until it says what they want it to instead of reading it and taking it to mean exactly what it says."

"Right. Or explain it away."

"True. Sometimes I wonder how they can do that. It's not like God's up there scratching His head somewhere going, what was I thinking about that whole hellfire raining down on Sodom and Gomorrah? Man, I can't believe I destroyed two whole cities. I just didn't know they weren't really sinning. Oops."

She laughed, a little humorlessly, because it was so obviously true. People turned God into what they wanted Him to be, instead of turning themselves into what God wanted *them* to be.

"I'm guilty of that," Keene said. "Just so you know. I try not to do it, but I can't point my finger at other people without saying that I'm guilty of all of those things. I could get caught up in the idea of wanting the government to come rescue me. Wanting to take the easy way out. Of not wanting to change and do the hard things, of wanting an easier version of Christianity than the one I know God intends for us."

"I think we all are. I am too." She seemed to have relaxed beside him, no longer afraid as the tractor moved along. Every once in a while, they'd hit a bump, and she'd reach for the armrest, but she was no longer sitting ramrod straight and jerking her head around at every little thing.

They weren't exactly having a relaxing conversation, but she was the one who broke the silence.

"You know, the things that God wants us to do sometimes seem hard. A lot of times, they seem hard. And they seem to go against our natural inclinations. But we know God, that He wouldn't command us to do anything that wasn't the very best for us."

"Sometimes I don't understand how the things that He tells us to do could possibly be the best for us, but I agree. Somehow, they are. Sometimes we're just too low to the ground, we don't have an omnipotent view of the world, or of eternity, to understand how the things that He commands are best."

"That's where faith comes in."

"I agree."

They rode in silence for a while as he made his way back down the lane, widening their driveway, keeping the blade up just a little so he wouldn't tear the stones off of theirs either.

Every once in a while, the wind would whip down, mostly coming from the west, and it blew the snow around the cab, swirling and blinding, and for several seconds they might not be able to see.

When that happened, Shelby's knuckles would go white, and she seemed to hold her breath until the snow cleared and they could see their way again.

"That's faith too," she eventually said.

It didn't seem to apply to anything that they'd been talking about, so he slowed down to steer around the mailbox and turn around before saying, "What?"

"Driving in the blinding whiteout. Just keeping the wheel straight and believing that what you just saw before everything went white is what you're going to see when everything clears up again."

"Yeah. That's true. I suppose that's a lot like life. You just keep going—even when you can't see your way sometimes. And also, like life, it gets easier the more you do it."

"I noticed that. Doesn't even seem to bother you that you can't see where we're going. And it just drives me crazy."

"Yeah. I've done it for years, and I was with my dad in the tractor when he did it. There are just some times when you can't see. And you have to go by faith."

"I guess this might be a good time to talk about the thing you suggested a couple of days ago."

"The Thing?" he said, a lot of teasing in his voice.

He started back up the driveway before she spoke again. "Yes. The Thing. I'm sorry, it's a little bit..."

"Awkward?"

"Yeah. Maybe. Because, well, because I don't know exactly what you're thinking."

"It shouldn't matter, should it?"

"I suppose you're right. It probably shouldn't, but it does. I don't want to make a fool out of myself, for no reason anyway."

"I'm pretty sure there's nothing you could do that would make you look foolish in my eyes."

"Oh, trust me. I could really make myself look dumb. I'm actually kind of good at it."

"I'll take your word for it."

"If you're around me very much, you'll experience it. Trust me."

"Okay. I believe you."

"That was easy."

"I feel like maybe I need to save up my arguments for the things that really matter."

"Okay. That's strategy. I'm impressed. I don't usually go into conversations with strategies."

"This is a conversation that I want to go in a certain direction. Normally I don't try to manipulate them, but I definitely have an endgame in mind, and maybe it's the male in me, but I'm playing to win."

Chapter 22

He gave her a side-look, knowing his confidence wasn't nearly as high as what he made it sound. "I hope you know that to me, a win for me is a win for both of us. I don't think I'm winning and you're losing. I think if we do the right thing, we're both gonna win. And I'm not just saying that as some mumbo-jumbo trying to talk anyone into anything. I'm being serious and honest."

"I didn't think you were. But we can't see the future. We don't know what the best thing is."

"We can make an educated guess. Based on what we know to be true."

"I know, but is that how we really want to decide to get married? An educated guess based on previous facts?"

"What's the other option?"

"You fall in love with someone. You have feelings for them. You can't get them off your mind or out of your heart. You want them more than anyone else."

She looked straight ahead while she was talking and then out the side window and away from him.

And it made him realize that maybe he'd been going about everything all wrong. He liked her, and he wanted her, and he felt like he'd given her an option that would help her to choose him.

But he'd forgotten that men and women were different, and she didn't want to make the sensible choice, not in her heart.

In her heart, she wanted romance. Pretty words. Grand gestures. All the little things that made a woman feel like a man wanted her, cared about her above all others, and when given a choice, would choose her. Didn't want anyone but her.

And here he'd been trying to make it about practicality. About solving her need for a place to stay and hoping that he could provide for her so she didn't have to work so hard.

So she'd have more time to spend with her children. So that she could be a mom and maybe even do some things that would make her feel like she was making a contribution in the world, like if she wanted to go back and further her degree or work toward getting a job that would be a little more satisfying than what she was currently doing.

He had thought he was offering good things.

But he'd missed the point.

Funny how it had to slam him in the forehead.

"See?" she said. "I knew I would say things and make myself look dumb."

"No. Actually, you said things and made me see where I had messed up."

They had reached the house again, and he stopped the tractor where the driveway branched off to go to the house or to the barns a hundred yards beyond.

"Do you mind if we go in for a minute? It's not like they're going to be shocked to see us, but I usually walk in and chat for a minute or two before I finish up."

"Of course. I'd love to."

"Let me go first, please," he said, tilting the steering wheel up, before he reached over and opened the door.

"Of course," she said, leaning back so he could cross over in front of her and go down the steps.

He turned around, figuring that he probably wasn't going to be able to get the pretty words and all the other stuff right in the romance considering he had exactly zero practice in pretty words and not much in romance, but he could maybe be a little bit gallant if he really put his mind to it.

Turning around, he met her eyes as she stood, leaning over and grabbing a hold of the handle before carefully putting her boot on the top step.

"Mind if I help you?" he asked, figuring she probably wouldn't say no but still feeling like it was a risk.

"I'm pretty sure you can tell by the way I look that I need all the help I can get."

"That wasn't really what I was thinking," he said as she came down a step, and his hands slid under the coat she was wearing and around her waist, steadying her.

Her eyes flew to his. Maybe she wasn't quite expecting the whole under the coat thing although his hands were firmly on top of her sweatshirt.

"Then, what were you thinking?" she asked, coming down another step and then landing with her foot on the ground, her face tilted up toward his.

"I was thinking...I wanted to touch you. I wanted an excuse to be close to you. I wanted you to know that I wasn't just suggesting something practical. That... I'm probably not any good at romance, but that's how I feel about you. Like I want to be good at it. For you."

His words weren't what he wanted them to be, but her eyes twitched, and her mouth opened just slightly, like maybe even though he felt like everything he was saying was not worthwhile, she understood, and it meant something to her.

"Oh."

That's all. Maybe she was speechless; whether that was because she liked what he said or because he was the most romantically incompetent man she'd ever been around, he wasn't sure.

Maybe he'd better get clear on that. "Was that a good oh? Or was that an oh, this man needs a lot of help if he ever hopes to be even slightly competent at romancing the woman whom he's interested in kind of oh?"

"The first," she said thoughtfully. "If you're talking about me? Talking about romancing me? Then, anything that comes from your heart because you...want me, is perfect."

"My words were far from perfect. Even I could tell that. But, in my defense, I haven't practiced on anyone, and so you're dealing with a beginner."

"I think you're a natural."

He laughed outright at that. "I know I'm not. But some people have said that I learn quickly. I might not learn fast enough, but I want to. Interest is a great teacher."

"Interest? In romance?"

"Yeah. And you. Interest in you."

Her breath caught, and maybe it was too soon, maybe he was pushing things, but he stepped forward, his head lowering, watching her eyes darken as his hand slid around her waist and pulled her closer.

"Keene! You don't usually have a rider with you." Meg McCartney, the eldest of the McCartney sisters, came around the tractor.

Keene didn't exactly jerk back, but he did lift his head although his hands stayed around Shelby's waist. Maybe she tugged just a little to step back, but his eyes held hers, wanting her to know that he wanted this too. It wasn't just a matter of convenience or practicality.

This might not have been exactly the kind of romance she wanted, but he figured part of romance was letting other people know that he wanted her. Or, way beyond that, that he wanted to be with her, that he would do things he didn't normally do for her, that he would risk rejection just to let others know where he stood with her.

At least, he thought that was what romance was. A part of it.

Her eyes softened, and her lips turned up ever so slightly. He considered that a good thing and turned toward Meg, who, if she were surprised to see him not only riding with someone but in a rather romantic-looking embrace, didn't let on.

"You guys were out here so long, I wasn't sure whether you were going to come into the house or not. I threw some hot chocolate on the stove, but there's coffee too." She shot a knowing look at Keene, and he grinned.

"Thanks. If it's okay with Shelby, we'll step in for a bit. Not long, though, because once we get your barn plowed out, I've got some things around the farm I wanted to do as well." Although, he mostly didn't want to spend all the kid-free time he had with Shelby talking to someone else.

"Of course. Any visit would be great. Are you going to introduce me to your friend?"

Maybe it was just his imagination, but she seemed to put a little bit of interesting emphasis on "friend." Like maybe she was teasing him—as old friends have a tendency of doing to each other.

"I'd love to. This is Shelby Yingling. You knew her in school as Shelby Henniger. Her roof caved in because of the snow, and she and her children and her mom are staying at the farmhouse."

"With you? Aren't you there by yourself? If I remember correctly, this was the week that your gram was going to be having surgery, right? At least I thought that was who Candace was making a meal for the other day."

"Yeah. Preston's taking care of her at her house, and that's where I'm staying at night."

"Wow." Meg's eyes widened. "You're pretty brave to be staying at the farm by yourself; it's awfully far out there." Meg shot an easy smile at Shelby as they started walking toward the house.

Someone had taken the time to make a nice wide path, but it was still only wide enough for two abreast.

Meg walked ahead while Shelby and Keene followed behind. His hands had fallen off her waist, but she hadn't objected to that, so he put his arm around her shoulder as they walked, grateful when she didn't try to shrug it off.

He wanted to finish their conversation, but he didn't want to be rude to their neighbor, and he always walked in for coffee and a little bit of conversation before he finished plowing.

Meg chattered about the weather and the storm, reaching the back steps and stomping her boots off as she climbed them. She opened the door and said over her shoulder, "Don't worry about taking your boots off. We've been going in and out all day, and I'll clean the kitchen up this evening."

He appreciated that, which was the way it usually was when he was here. No one had time to tie and untie their boots when coming in.

It'd be different if they were coming to visit and going to sit in the living room or something.

It seemed to bother Shelby a little as she took some extra time knocking all the snow off her boots.

"It's okay. Really. Everybody's used to it. It's just what we do," he said softly, trying to ease a little of her anxiety.

She looked up. "Was I that obvious?"

He grinned. "I get it. Some people get really picky about their houses, but that's not the way we are around here. People are more important."

"Well, you keep your house clean because of people. You know, because it's pleasant to go into a nice clean room and much more relaxing than it is to go into a place that's dirty and you're not sure whether it's safe to eat anything there or not."

"Good point. I can't argue with that."

"Normally men don't notice when it's clean, though," she said, lowering her brows just a bit as though she wasn't expecting him to agree with her.

"I don't think women have the monopoly on cleanliness. I just think sometimes that's something that they're more likely to make an idol than men are. We're more likely to want to keep our tractor clean or our truck shined up, things of that nature."

She grinned, and he assumed she agreed, as she walked in while he held the door for her.

Chapter 23

"How's Esther doing?" Keene asked as he shut the door. He should have asked earlier but hadn't thought about it.

"The same. Doctors can't really say whether she'll ever be any better. But we just take it a day at a time."

Shelby gave him a confused look, like she didn't know what they're talking about. Meg must have read her look and opened her mouth before he could.

"Esther had what they thought was Lyme disease. But it's not acting the way that normal cases do. She just...hasn't had any energy and seems to get every infection under the sun. She's constantly sick. She hasn't been able to work, and doctors can't help her. Antibiotics don't touch it, and they said there's just nothing they can do other than keep an eye on her and make sure they treat any secondary infections."

"Oh, that's terrible," Shelby said, sounding horrified, and he could almost read her mind where she was wondering if something like that might happen to her children.

He wanted to reassure her that this was one of those one-in-a-million things that most people would most certainly never experience and many would never hear about. But Meg was talking again.

"She's sleeping right now, which is what she's normally doing, or I'd say she'd probably appreciate you going and talking to her. She doesn't get a whole lot of visitors. At first, a lot of people came, but it's been dragging on for so long that I think people just get busy with other things."

"I'm guilty. I have to make time to come and see her more often. I hadn't really thought that she might be lonely."

"I think she probably is. But more, she feels like her life is passing by and there's not a lot she can do about it."

"It's an especially hard time of year to be down," Shelby said.

Meg agreed, bringing two cups of hot chocolate and setting them down on the table along with Keene's coffee.

From there, Keene felt like an extraneous item of kitchen décor, as the two ladies were soon chatting like old friends. Christmas, sisters, children, farms, snow, and being brave in a farmhouse when one was alone were all topics they touched on.

Keene buried his nose in his coffee and didn't even bother trying to keep up. By the time he'd figure out what they were talking about, they be onto a different subject.

Finally, his coffee had been drunk for a good five minutes when he stood and said, "I think we'd better go out and get the rest of this driveway plowed."

If he didn't get Shelby back in the tractor with him, he wasn't going to have any more time to talk to her by herself. Preston would be back with her kids and her mom, and his opportunity would be gone.

Funny that he felt so possessive over her time and wanted it all for himself.

They waved goodbye as Meg walked them to the door. He waited until it shut behind them before he said, "I should have offered to go ahead and plow while you two stayed in and talked. You guys seemed like you were having a really great time, and it was a little selfish of me to assume that you'd want to come back out with me instead of staying."

"I'd forgotten how sweet she was. And I was really grateful for the opportunity to visit, but I'd rather be with you."

Maybe she said the last line a little shyly, like she wasn't sure whether she could admit it, and he wondered if maybe part of that had to do with some of her admiration being misplaced with her previous husband.

Like she had admired him and had wanted to be with him, while he had taken advantage of that and not returned her feelings.

"I'm glad, because I wanted to take you out about three minutes after we went in. Just because I wanted to have you to myself. But I didn't want to be rude."

She smiled at the compliment, at the idea that he wanted her, and he thought that maybe he was doing okay with the whole romance thing. It was just basically trying to figure out how to put his feelings into words in a way that he would be able to say it without sounding ridiculous.

He waited until they were on the other side of the tractor, out of sight of the house, before he took her hand.

He tugged her to a stop, right beside the steps, and put one of his booted feet up on one step while he pulled her closer.

"I feel like maybe we got interrupted, and I was hoping you might have been as disappointed as I was."

She smiled and tilted her head. "Maybe."

He grinned, liking that she was flirting with him a little.

"I wasn't really talking about...about the fact that I had wanted to kiss you before we went in. I was talking about the conversation."

Her smile didn't fade. And he figured that was because he had admitted to wanting to kiss her. She seemed okay with it.

"You were talking about...romance. And how what I had suggested was lacking. And I know you're right. I had admitted I wasn't very good at it, and I just wanted you to know that maybe I kind of made the whole proposition sound like a business idea, where you need a place to stay and I'm ready to settle down, and it all seemed kind of cut and dried without any emotion in it. And emotion isn't exactly my greatest ability, but I wanted you to know that I'll try. Because I'm not thinking about this like a business proposition. I'm thinking about it like getting married makes the most sense, but I'm not trying to shortcut all the things that you were supposed to have. The pretty words, the grand gestures, the devotion, the loyalty, and being my priority."

Just saying all of those things scared him a little. "I...I'm not going to do all of those things perfectly, and I hope you bear with me while I get better at them. But I just wanted you to know that's what I'm thinking."

"Thank you. Thank you so much for hearing what I was saying and knowing what I needed. I appreciate you not just realizing it but taking steps immediately to do something about it. That really means a lot."

"I want to do this right. Maybe a little fast, but right."

"Do you remember when my roof caved in and I had just talked to Miss Ginny and she said anything that happens could be the best thing that ever happens to you? With you being mostly gone the last two days and with me not going to work, I've had a lot of time to think. It seems like everything happens for a reason and God pulls all the parts of your life together just whenever they need to be. Getting that advice, having my roof cave in, having you suggest that...that we get married....it just all seems to be working out, and as crazy as it sounds, I don't have any qualms about saying yes. And walking into that. And what you just did today just confirms everything I've been thinking. That I'm not really taking a risk with you. Instead, I'm reaching out and grabbing a hold of something that God is giving me that is better than anything I could have ever imagined." She bit her lip while she looked up, searching his face. "You haven't changed your mind?"

Her question made him smile, and he bent his head, brushing his lips over her forehead. "Not a chance. If anything, I want it more today than I did two days ago. The heart of me wants it more. My brain was already sold on it being a really great idea, and my heart was on board, but now, it's kind of taken the lead if that makes sense."

"It does. And that was...almost romantic."

"Almost? Man. You have high standards."

"Sorry. Let me rephrase. That was beautifully romantic."

"So which is true? The first one or the second?"

"Both." She grinned. "This is where you kiss me so I don't have to try to explain that comment."

He laughed. "That's a really good way to win an argument. I think I'm going to let you." He was still grinning as he lowered his head, and so was she. It made for a little bit of teeth clacking, as teeth met before lips did, but he turned his head a little, and she moved closer, and soon everything fit perfectly together.

Chapter 24

That evening, Keene walked into the kitchen to the scent of fresh-baked bread and something that smelled an awful lot like a hearty beef stew.

"I'll plow snow all day long every day if I get to come into a kitchen that smells this good every evening." His eyes met Shelby's over Perry's head as she sat him in his booster seat. Grace carried butter and a knife to the table while Haley carried something that looked like applesauce.

Cindi was already sitting at the table, spooning out a little of the stew into Perry's plate to cool.

Shelby looked serene and content although there might have been a little extra pink in her cheeks. Maybe she wasn't thinking about their kiss earlier in the day, but he sure was. It made his lips curve up and his heart beat faster. It also made him hope a little that the kids were worn out from playing in the snow all afternoon and would be ready for bed immediately after they ate.

That was wishful thinking, he was pretty sure, but still a nice thought.

"I can't let you get ahead of me in the romance department," Shelby said, and yeah, there was most definitely pink in her cheeks.

His brows went up. He supposed any kind of competition would get him going, but he loved the idea of competing about who could be the most romantic.

She lifted her chin in a challenge. He almost said, "Accepted," but he didn't want to have to explain what he was talking about to the kids who were almost certain to ask.

Instead, he placed his boots on the boot dryer and walked on stockinged feet across the kitchen, feeling a little like he was stalking the woman he wanted.

Why not?

He didn't stop until he had one hand around her waist and her eyes were wide with surprise. She still held the spoon that she'd been stirring the soup on the stove with.

"This isn't romance, exactly. This is just me not being able to see you without wanting to kiss you." His words were low and a little slow as he held her gaze.

She smiled before he finished speaking, and he figured that meant she was okay. He lowered his head but didn't kiss her nearly as long as he wanted to, what with all the other people in the kitchen.

"Keene?" she said, and he bit back a satisfied smile at how breathless she sounded.

"Yeah?" He wasn't as dismayed as he should have been over how breathless his own voice was.

"Maybe we could fix this thing between us so you don't have to leave in the evenings anymore?"

The smile he'd successfully bitten back, escaped, but she didn't seem to be offended. If anything, her smile matched it. Probably because of his reaction.

"Tomorrow?" he asked, low.

"Yes, if we can't do it tonight."

"The courthouse closes at five. It's six now."

"Then, tomorrow."

"What's happening tomorrow?" Grace's voice cut through the chatter that had been going on around the table with the kids and Cindi.

"Your mother is going to make an honest man of me and allow me to move back into my house."

"Oh?" Shelby said, with a raised brow.

He had been teasing, and he figured she was, too, since her look wasn't the slightest bit serious, but he also figured this was a good time for him to practice being romantic.

Announcing his feelings in front of people wasn't exactly high on his list of things he wanted to do; but complimenting the woman he loved in front of her children seemed like a good romantic gesture. Public compliments, kind words that lifted someone up and encouraged them and brought positive attention to them in front of other people couldn't be discounted, and with the things that Shelby had suffered with her husband and his leaving, she could use a lot of building up.

"Grace. And Haley and Perry. Cindi, too. I love your mother. Your daughter. I love her work ethic. Her diligence. Her devotion to her family and her sense of humor. I love that she doesn't cast blame but plows forward, doing the best she can with what she has. I love her smile, her positive outlook, her laugh, and her determination to do the hard things." He tugged her back against him and she went willingly. Maybe her eyes were a little misty, but it was a good mist. "And I'm honored and excited that she's agreed to marry me. Tomorrow."

His eyes met Cindi's over the heads of the children. So help him, she was teary-eyed, too. He took that as permission. He hadn't even considered asking her if it was okay. Maybe that was a little old-fashioned, but it was always a good idea.

"Does that mean you'll be our dad?" Haley didn't exactly seem upset, but she didn't seem happy, either.

"If you want. If you're more comfortable not, that's fine, too."

"What about Daddy?" Grace asked, and Keene got the impression she was more interested in getting rid of the man who had left her mother than she was concerned about someone else taking his place.

"Nothing is changing with him. He's always been welcome to come see you. Always. And if he wants you to go see him...we'll talk about it." Shelby spoke firmly. The kind of tone that didn't allow room for arguments or discussion.

"Are we attending the wedding?" Cindi asked, her eyes still moist.

"Of course. I couldn't do this without my family." Shelby smiled at the people at the table who were looking at her and Keene like they held the world.

Which, for the kids, especially, they pretty much did.

"And I'm marrying your mom, but I want you all, too," Keene said so there wasn't any doubt. Cindi had looked uncertain, like she wasn't sure if she was wanted or needed.

Her next words confirmed it. "I can try to find somewhere else to live. You need some privacy as newlyweds."

"No."

Shelby and Keene spoke together, then Shelby looked up at him, love shining in her eyes.

"I want you here. When I asked Shelby to marry me, I knew she came with all of you, and that's what I want. Everyone."

"I love you." Shelby wasn't looking at her family; her gaze, which Keene almost thought was adoring, was focused on him.

"I love you, too." Keene grinned. "Just in case you didn't hear me telling your family that earlier."

"I didn't miss it, but I don't mind hearing it over and over. And over."

"I'll keep that in mind."

The wind gusted, rattling the panes in the windows and making the kitchen seem even more warm and cozy.

"Now. Can a man get a taste of everything that has been seducing his nose since he stepped in the kitchen? Oh. I forgot to say I love that your mother is a great cook," he quipped at the children.

"You haven't even tried it yet. And this is the first time in my life I've made bread. It might be terrible."

"The kids said you were good. I'll take their word for it. And if you need some instruction, I'm sure Grace and Haley will be happy to help you out."

The girls giggled, and Shelby's mouth trembled. Loving her children and her mother might not count as romance. Not in a romance book or a movie on TV, but if he knew Shelby, protecting and taking care of her family would be better romance than a thousand boxes of chocolate or vases of flowers. He'd rather have a woman who knew what was important in life and that was another thing he loved about her.

"I keep thinking of things I forgot to mention when I was telling everyone what I loved about you."

"Just break into the conversation and blurt them out. I'm fine with that." Shelby grinned as she moved away from him, putting the spoon back in the stew and giving it a stir. "And maybe I should start listing the things I love about you."

"Don't say them all at once. I want to savor it and enjoy it."

"Maybe I'll write them down and pin them to the refrigerator."

"And maybe I'll steal that list and put it in my wallet and carry it around with me."

"I'll make a copy for you."

He picked the pot of stew up and set it on the table. "I'll take you up on that. A list of things you love about me and a daily note. Letting me know that nothing has changed."

She nodded, and as they sat down together, he clasped her hand in his before his new family bowed their heads in unison and he asked the blessing.

Epilogue

Esther McCartney lay on the couch in the big farmhouse where she'd grown up.

Exhausted.

As she'd been for more than a year.

She was sick and tired of being sick and tired. But no medicine had seemed to help, and the doctors had told her that maybe her body just needed time to heal itself.

She'd begged them to tell her how long it would take to get better, but no one had an answer for her.

From the pitying looks they'd cast over their shoulders as the people in long white lab coats whispered in a group in the corner about her condition, she half wondered if she'd ever get better.

"Hello, the house!" a familiar male voice called.

Not familiar because he was here to see her. Not too many people were still coming to visit. It had been a year. Most folks thought she should be better by now. Sometimes, Esther figured they thought she was faking it or milking her disability out.

Like she'd ever choose to stay in bed.

She'd been an athlete—and a good one—in school. A farm girl, and she loved it. Involved in her church and community and heady with the pleasure of living life. Like she'd ever voluntarily remove herself from everything she loved.

"Come on in, Monroe," she said, hating the tiredness in her voice.

"Hey, Moxie." The door closed. There were footsteps, then Monroe's head appeared in the doorway.

"Candace is still at the barn. She texted me, said she tried to text you but you didn't answer." Monroe dated Candace on-again-off-again. They were more like good friends than boyfriend/girlfriend, but neither of them had better prospects, so they kept at it. It was Saturday night, and he was here for their weekly date.

Sometimes, he came early and chatted with her for a bit, but he was late tonight.

"I didn't get it. I dropped my phone in the toilet."

She giggled, despite her tiredness. "Please tell me it's still there."

"Nope." He walked over, pulling the chair he always sat in when they visited, waiting for Candace to get ready, and setting it in the spot he always did, right beside her. "I reached in, swirling the water because I figured if I was going to have my hand in the toilet, I might as well clean it. Why waste a good thing, right?"

"You're lying."

"Yeah. I dropped it in the water trough. But I figured you'd laugh if I told you it was the toilet."

"You lied!"

"To make you laugh. God told me it was okay."

"He did not. And that's blasphemy."

Monroe came from a family of almost all boys, except for one little sister, Catherine, whom they'd basically ignored for most of her life. Esther had never had the nerve to bring the sister up and ask why Monroe hadn't made more of an effort to include her in the family. And she figured it wasn't any of her business anyway.

He'd been nice to her, and she appreciated it, but it was Candace in whom he was interested.

"You're right. I did it because of my own sinful nature. But God really does have a sense of humor."

"I don't doubt it. He made you," Esther said dryly. "And you just lied about playing in the toilet-"

"I didn't lie about playing! I was working. Didn't you hear me say I took the opportunity to clean it?"

"You don't clean toilets with your bare hands."

"Maybe you don't."

"Maybe no one does. No one except eight-year-old boys who don't know any better."

"I've been accused of never growing up. Maybe that's what they meant." Monroe looked thoughtful.

"I can almost guarantee it."

That was another thing about Monroe. He never asked how she felt. Like he knew if she felt better, she wouldn't be lying on the couch.

"Hey, guys! Sorry I'm late." Candace spoke from the doorway, sounding out of breath, like she'd run in from the barn.

"Take your time. I'm busy now anyway," Monroe said, grinning and winking at Esther.

"You have an audience who can't escape, so you can practice your comedy routine all you want, and she's completely at your mercy."

Esther swallowed and tried to smile. She hated being reminded that she wasn't well. Although, she also knew that Candace didn't mean anything by it.

"I don't think Esther will ever be at anyone's mercy. She might be down, but she's far from out."

"You're right, Monroe." Candace stuck her head in the doorway, half of a boiled egg in her hand. "Esther's always been better company than me anyway. Even flat out, she always has a comeback."

"That's true. Hey! I thought we were going out to eat. Your turn to pay." Monroe's brows lowered. "You'd better not think you're getting away with being cheap and taking me to a hot dog stand or something."

"I like hotdogs," Candace said with her mouth full.

"For an appetizer," Monroe mumbled, glancing at Esther who mouthed, "Make her take you to Chester's."

He grinned. Chester's was the most expensive restaurant in a hundred-mile radius.

They exchanged a humorous glance at each other before Esther called out, "He wants to go to Chester's."

Candace, who was back in the kitchen, her mouth still full, said, "Wonderful. Now I'm going to have to share my boiled eggs with him, or I'll go broke buying his dinners."

"Maybe you should have offered in the first place instead of coming in here and flaunting your food while the rest of us could only drool." Esther wrinkled her nose. She hated boiled eggs.

"You hate boiled eggs," Monroe whispered.

"You hate boiled eggs," Candace called.

"But I haven't eaten since breakfast!" She tried to look pitiful, and Monroe didn't seem to know whether to believe that or not.

"Neither have I. That's why I needed the boiled eggs, so I didn't pass out from low blood sugar until we get where we're going. Monroe drives slower than a turtle in Park."

"You've just officially offended me."

"You'll get over it as soon as you get the menu from Chester's in your hand." Candace walked in and handed them both a boiled egg. "I'm going to get a shower. You really want Chester's? I'll have to dig something other than jeans and a sweatshirt out of my closet."

"Borrow something from Esther. She's got great taste." Monroe held his hand out and Esther gave him her egg.

"Good idea. She's not going to be using it anytime soon anyway."

Esther tried to keep the hurt that comment elicited from showing on her face. "You can't wear my white blouse with the black buttons."

"That's the one I was going for. It's perfect for Chester's."

Monroe took a look at Esther's face and swallowed his egg before he called out, "Wear your green shirt. The one with the gold stuff on it. That looks good on you."

"I don't have a green shirt." Candace's voice sounded confused.

Monroe looked panicked.

"Tell her to wear the blue one. It brings out the blue of her eyes."

"Wear the blue one. It brings out the blue of your eyes."

"Really? You like that one?"

Esther nodded, prompting Monroe.

"Yeah. I like it a lot." He lifted his hands, popping the last of her egg in his mouth before he whispered, "What blue one? I don't remember that one."

"Trust me," Esther said. "It's her favorite."

"Oh."

"That's my favorite," Candace called down. "I'm glad you like it."

They shared conspiring grins.

The whole exchange had tired Esther, and she focused on not nodding off while Monroe talked a bit about his day and what had caused him to drop his phone in the water trough.

Maybe it was just her imagination that she always felt better after Monroe visited and always had more energy while he was there. Maybe she just enjoyed him and appreciated that he seemed to know what bothered her and what didn't and was able to chat without making her feel like the almost-invalid she was.

Regardless, Monroe and Candace, for all their relaxed dating, would probably end up married one of these years, starting a family while she languished on the couch. The aunt who wasn't any fun.

It was a dismal prospect.

~~~

Thanks so much for reading! If you'd like to read the next book in A Heartland Cowboy Christmas, *Heartland Giving*, you can get it HERE[1].

If you'd like to interact with me, join my Facebook group[2].

I'd love for you to sign up for my newsletter[3] to read about my daily life on the farm, be the first to know about my new releases, get deals on my books and occasionally get other sweet romance deals as well.

---

1. https://www.amazon.com/gp/product/B09HRLDJD8

2.   https://www.facebook.com/groups/jessiegussman/

3.   https://dl.bookfunnel.com/svgbc8n23d

~~~

Enjoy this preview of *Heartland Giving*, just for you!

Heartland Giving
Chapter 1

Esther McCartney pushed the grocery store cart in front of her, trying not to lean too heavily on it.

Grocery shopping had always been one of her least favorite chores, but not today. Today, she was celebrating the fact that she was actually in a grocery store.

It was the first time she'd been shopping in more than a year.

It felt like a huge victory, but she was already exhausted, and she hadn't even made it to the checkout line yet.

Checking her phone, making sure she'd gotten everything on the short list that her sisters had put together with her, she took a deep breath and started toward the self-checkout, wondering how she was going to get everything checked out and loaded in the car when all she felt like doing was lying down with her face on the floor and resting for several hours at least.

For her first outing in months, she should have been content to drive to Prairie Rose and take a letter to the post office or something.

But no, she had felt so well today she volunteered to go shopping.

After her sisters had gotten over their shock and Candace had voiced her disapproval, they had helped her figure out what they needed.

As the eldest, Candace felt like she was in charge most of the time.

Mostly they were happy for her—even if they were a little worried too.

For the last month, Esther had started on a new diet and a natural supplement regimen, and it had helped.

To the point where she felt like she could leave the farm and run an errand like grocery shopping.

She had been overly optimistic and probably should have listened to Candace, who had suggested she not do something quite so ambitious for her first excursion to town in close to a year.

She hated it when her elder sister was right.

Especially when that made her wrong.

Panting like she'd run a marathon instead of walked halfway around the grocery store putting less than 20 items in her cart, she leaned heavily on the handle as she turned the corner to go left toward the self-checkout. At least at the self-checkout, she could take as much time as she needed.

But her judgment was off, and she cut the corner too closely, clipping the edge of a carefully stacked pyramid of chocolate sandwich cookies, and the entire thing came tumbling down around her and her cart.

It was bad enough to destroy someone's hard work, but the noise reverberated so that everyone in the store was craning their necks to see what had happened.

Prairie Rose was a small town, and she'd already been stopped at least fifteen times by pretty much every shopper she passed, asking about her health.

It was one of her pet peeves of being sick, people asking her how she was. If she was well, she'd be doing a regular routine. Since she wasn't, she obviously didn't feel great, and she hated continually having to come up with words that didn't sound too negative. Like *yeah, I feel rotten, but I'm up anyway.* Or *yeah, I feel terrible, that's why I'm on the couch.*

Bending down to begin to pick up the containers of cookies that had fallen everywhere, she fought the fatigue and the nausea that weakened her knees even while her cheeks heated and embarrassment made her want to sink into the floor.

She wasn't so desperate for attention that she needed to knock down a display so everyone in the store would stop and look at her.

"Oh, don't worry about it. I'll get it." Tara, the teenage cashier that Esther had known since birth, panted as she hurried over, hot and sweaty, and knelt down to help.

"You can go back to your register. I'll help. You guys are already shorthanded because of everyone having off to get ready for the Christmas parade tonight." A deep voice, familiar, spoke just over Esther's head.

It wasn't one she particularly wanted to hear. Not when she was feeling like she could barely lift her hands and was kneeling in front of a huge mess that needed to be cleaned up.

"Are you sure, Monroe?" Tara said, relief in her tone but also a question.

"Yeah. I think we can stack these back the way they were without too much trouble, and that way the folks waiting in line won't be mad at us."

Tara nodded, giving Esther a smile and a wave before she hurried back to her register.

"Us?" Esther asked, the exhaustion in her voice making her want to cringe. "I don't recall seeing you around when I knocked it down."

"No one can ever tell the difference between you and your sister anyway. They'll just think we were together."

That was probably true. Candace, who had been casually dating Monroe for a while, looked almost exactly like Esther. Their personalities were completely different, but people often confused them, and when they were together, people asked if they were twins.

It really wasn't what she wanted people to think, though.

But she did appreciate the help.

"What are you doing out anyway? Are you and your sisters so desperate for groceries that you'll starve to death if you don't show up at the store?" Monroe asked, his tone low, as they knelt together picking up the packages. She doing it much slower than he.

"You know I've been feeling better since I started on those new supplements. But I think I might have bitten off more than I could chew."

She wouldn't have admitted that to just anyone, but Monroe had been at their house a good bit because of Candace. Often, while he was waiting for Candace to get ready, he sat and talked to Esther.

Sometimes he'd come to visit her, just because.

He was pretty much the only one; Esther had been confined to the house for so long that people seemed to have forgotten about her.

"Moxie," he said, using the nickname he'd started calling her after all the time they'd spent together while waiting for Candace to get ready.

She didn't look at him, focusing on getting the mess cleaned up with her last bit of energy. If she had to let her cart sit in the store, she would.

His hand settled on hers, and he said, "Moxie," more forcefully this time, and her hand stilled. She looked up.

"I've got this. You look like you're about ready to fall over. Go on and sit down on the bench on the other side of the cash registers. I'll get this, then I'll get your groceries, and then I'll help you out."

"No. Really. I can do this."

"Of course, you can. Eventually. But this is your first time out of the house in almost a year. You've already done enough. You're going to hurt yourself or hurt someone else."

She glared at him. Not wanting to hear the truth. But knowing he was right.

"All right, fine. You sit there. Let me do this. Then we'll check out together, okay?"

She didn't want her eyes to fill with tears. They weren't sad tears or weak tears; they were frustrated tears. She had been healthy and energetic and active all of her life. Why was she so weak and tired now?

Trust me. Every trial is for a reason.

She closed her eyes and said a quick prayer—*Help me, Lord*—before she relaxed her hands, putting them in her lap while she knelt on the floor. Resting. While Monroe picked up everything.

She'd fought her diagnosis, fought the exhaustion, fought everything that had been laid on her, and she wouldn't quit fighting, but at the same time, she could also accept that this whole trial was from the Lord. He wanted her to grow. Maybe to gain some compassion. She'd been trying.

"I would argue with you, but even if you give in, I can't really help you," she said, pushing the sour thoughts away, allowing her face to relax into a smile.

"That's my Moxie," Monroe said casually as his eyes lifted to hers and they shared a smile.

"When I feel better, I'm going to win an argument with you," she said, but her words lacked the force that she wanted to have behind them.

"You keep telling yourself that," he said, taking four packages in his hand and twisting them around, setting them down on the perfect pyramid he was building.

"You probably ought to slow down a little. You'll have the manager here wanting to hire you."

Monroe laughed. "Sometimes I think it would be better to work in a grocery store. I wouldn't be gone so much anyway."

Esther's eyes popped open. She hadn't realized being gone for long stretches of time bothered him. "I thought you liked touring the country?"

"I do. If I hadn't gotten to work on my dad's harvest crew, I wouldn't have been able to see nearly as much of it as what I have. But I guess it's always nice to come home to Iowa, and sometimes I do wish for regular hours and a regular schedule. Even though I love what I do."

He slapped another four packages carefully on the pyramid, then lifted his eyes to look at her.

They had talked enough that she knew exactly what he was saying. He had always spoken in glowing terms about his job, about how much he loved the wide-open skies, the feeling of friendship and pulling together he felt on the harvest crew. How he loved working for American farmers, and what a sense of pride it gave him to see the beauty of the country and knowing he was helping to feed it.

She had always been proud in the same way of the jobs she had. Of the hog barns they had that produced meat to supply to the country. When she wasn't being bitter and angry at her circumstances, she loved listening to Monroe talk about his experiences. Because she could relate—even if she did her part by just staying on their farm.

But she'd always been active and involved, and if she hadn't been laid up, she might have fiddled with the idea of hiring on to a harvest crew and seeing what it was all about.

Her sisters had managed the farm for the last year, almost completely without her help, so it was pretty obvious to her that although three people made the work lighter, they weren't necessary in order to run the farm.

A wave of dizziness made her sway, and her hand came up, grabbing Monroe's wide shoulder.

His head turned immediately. His brows lifted.

"You look like you're going to pass out." He put the packages down that he held in his hand and turned to her, taking both of her hands in his and standing. "Come on. Can you walk to the bench?"

His words were gentle. There was no censure or impatience. His touch was almost tender, and she found herself standing without protest.

"I know it would embarrass you if I carried you, but that's really what I want to do," Monroe murmured, putting his arm around her waist and allowing her to lean into his strength.

"I can do it," she said, hating the breathless gasps around the words and the empty feeling in her chest like she just didn't have any strength or air while her heart felt weak and anemic.

Monroe didn't say anything more but walked beside her as they passed the registers toward the bench.

Esther concentrated on putting one foot in front of another, but she didn't miss Tara's concerned glance as she looked up from where she was checking an elderly lady out.

"I'll get the rest of those in a minute. I wanted Esther to sit down for a bit," Monroe said, and Esther assumed Tara had given him a questioning glance.

She hated to be the center of attention in such a terrible way, but she also felt grateful that he was helping her over. He was right. She was on the verge of passing out. It would be worse to be flat out on the floor in the middle of the grocery store than it was to be helped to a bench.

You can continue reading by getting *Heartland Giving* HERE[1].

---

1. https://www.amazon.com/gp/product/B09HRLDJD8

Made in the USA
Columbia, SC
14 August 2022

64747274R00096